NORDIC
VAMPIRE ASSASSIN
LEAGUE

INCLUDES:
DEARLY BELOVED
FOREVER AS ONE

Jackie Ivie

A Vampire Assassin League
Novella

Dearly Beloved

JACKIE IVIE

CHAPTER ONE

The first indication something had gone wrong was the loud thump through the water that shoved her against the cave wall. The next was lack of air. Then her light died.

Courtney had a nanosecond of reaction time before the panic arrived, turning her world into one huge hell of rapidly increasing heart-beats and swiftly churning legs.

She'd known not to trust Shawn! That weasel brother-in-law of hers got her into more scrapes with more denizens of righteousness and physics than anyone could imagine, and if this was another of his stupid video pranks...

A dark shape flitted through the mass of opacity outlining the cave mouth, stilling her movements, but not her heart-rate. She didn't have time for worry over a shark attack. Not now. Courtney wasn't a deep diver for a reason. She couldn't hold her breath for the required three minutes. She'd barely made the one minute mark last night when Shawn talked her into this, and that was without panic factored in. *Besides*... Courtney gripped the handle of her spear gun with renewed confidence. She had a weapon equipped with a razor-honed spear. All she'd have to do is aim. And that she was an expert at.

But first, she had to have air!

She'd been in the mouth of the cave, but that still seemed to take an eternity to evacuate. From there, it was a short twenty-odd foot sprint to the surface and Shawn's yacht. And then she'd be aiming this spear at the belly of the crewman who'd just scared the bee-jeebers out of her. Because that's what she thought of Shawn's lame e-videos.

She took a peek upward to where moonlight should be silhouetting a dark shaped boat above her and got nothing but debris. Not much of it looked to have dimension or size, either…nothing recognizable as a fully equipped yacht or five men. If she hadn't needed every bit of air for survival, she'd have gasped. As it was, she barely stopped the impulse, by turning it into a mass corkscrew of movement for the surface.

Something grabbed an ankle, yanking her down into certain death. And that's when she turned and shot it.

o0o

That woman *shot* him.

Dominick yanked the metal spike from his side with a howl that reverberated through the density of ocean around them. She'd shot him. Him! And with a spike that would've killed had she hit him accurately. It still hurt. It also hampered his motions and pricked at his male pride, as well as made an easy-to-follow trail back through the cave that led to his home. That spike also marked her as a Hunter, changing everything about a simple assassination into a morass of treachery and betrayal and gut-wrenching anger. Those he'd deal with in their proper time...after he got her exactly where he wanted her, and in exactly what position.

Dominick pulled at the slender figure, bringing her against him for the lunge to his grotto. He needed answers and for that he needed her alive. And the woman needed air. Fresh air, sucked down to the seabed from his villa by a shaft he'd designed and then constructed. Dom had planned, designed, and over-seen every phase of every bit of construction on his villa. He was good with his hands. Usually.

He'd have to amend that in future. He wasn't good enough, or he'd have been able to stop the crewman from firing a bullet right through Dominick and into the tank behind him, ruining not only a supremely planned and orchestrated kill, but the resultant feast he'd planned, as well.

So now he had her. The woman who'd shot him.

He'd thought her an eel at first glance. It was easy to see why. She was covered in a full-body, tight, black wet-suit and she was overly thin. Stupid. The women in this time were short-sighted and ill-used; starving themselves into caricatures of the feminine form. Not only did that alter and subdue curves, but it also changed their blood offering into little more than weak, noxious-tasting fluid.

It was stupid and plain short-sighted, as he'd already noted. Not one of them would hold their own against a wench from the century of his spawning. Women nowadays were weak and getting weaker by the day. And yet, the Hunters actually recruited, trained, and came painfully close to succeeding by using one?

It didn't make sense, and by Lucifer, he was going to find out why.

The girl wasn't conscious anymore and she was at full dead-weight. If he didn't rush, she was just going to be full dead. Dominick wrapped both arms about her form and shot through the water, going air-borne above his pool within moments, before dropping to his feet. Then he was on his knees, placing the woman gingerly at the edge, pondering not only the vagaries of fate that had given him a Hunter - and a female one at that - but also the odd notion that he'd have to figure out how to bring a human back to life. He'd seen it in films but never attempted it. It had something to do with pushing at them and then pumping at their chest. With as light a motion as he could. With his strength, he'd likely meld her flesh right into the marble-covered pool deck. Maybe he'd be better served rolling her onto her belly and tapping at her back until she emptied out the ocean water she'd breathed in.

This was incomprehensible. Then it was laughable, and then it was work.

o0o

"Oh my God. What is this?" Courtney choked, inhaled liquid, and then coughed until it felt like a rib fractured. Actually...it felt more like two of them. If she'd cheated death, it hurt. And if she was dead and this was her eternity, then it really hurt.

"Drink. Now."

The voice was masculine and threatening, with a foreign tone to it and not one other bit of inflection.

Her entire frame rippled with the immediate shiver. She didn't think of disobeying, and took another gulp with the same coughing spasm, even as she decided it was just brandy. Maybe even cognac. It didn't really matter. She wasn't a connoisseur, and there were a lot more things to worry over. Things like where the devil was she? And with whom? And why did it feel like she was floating on pillows?

She opened her eyes and then lost the ability to do anything more. The god Apollo was sitting right next to her. In the flesh. That answered one portion of it. She'd obviously died and gone to Mount Olympus - or wherever the gods hung out nowadays. Which did mean pain was going to be part of this eternity of hers. Since Apollo here might be a part of it, pain was perfectly fine with her. Courtney blinked. Nothing about him changed. She was facing the epitome of a Grecian god, only this one was beyond handsome, with thick black hair, probing dark eyes, kiss-inducing lips, and since he was wearing a thinly-spun, white linen shirt, there wasn't anything hiding one hell of a physique. That was just his upper body. The liquor had already stolen her breath, or she'd have lost it along with a jaw-drop. As it was, her lip sagged and brandy spilled. Then he was on his feet and leaning forward, looming over her and sending shivers again as he dabbed at her lower lip with a cloth of some kind.

"I said drink. Not dribble."

"Who...are you?"

"I ask the questions. Not you."

Ok. So, maybe he wasn't Apollo, but he was damn close. Especially now that she could check out his lower frame, molded as it was by tan-colored slacks that weren't leaving much muscle and strength to the imagination, either.

"All right then. Shoot."

He pulled back as if she'd literally shot something, and a strange look came across such handsome features, she felt giddy and then faint. That just changed to giggles, spurting brandy-laced fumes up her nose, where it frothed and burned, making her feel worse than an idiot. She just wished that was all she felt. The response also sent spikes of ache as her chest revolted. All because a man handsome enough to stop traffic was back to leaning over her, propped on taut, sculpted arms as he studied her. Mortification was probably in these reactions somewhere, too, but for the life of her, she couldn't dredge it up just yet.

"How did you find me?"

"Find…you?" Pain chopped the words. It also made her grimace.

"Yes. Find me."

Courtney sent back a swallow that was more a gulp. He took it in with unblinking dark eyes shadowed by such thick dark lashes, they looked unreal. What was she thinking? The entire thing was unreal and it was getting difficult to pay attention. She hoped it was the effects from her near-drowning mixed with straight shots of brandy, and not from close proximity to Apollo, here. But that was probably wishful thinking. She wrinkled her brow in thought.

"I didn't."

"You did not what?"

"Find…anyone."

"You are here."

"I'm…really tired." The words limped out.

"Answer the question."

"Sleepy…"

"I need to know how you found me and by what method. You are not allowed rest until you tell me."

This made less sense than before. Unless he really was Apollo and she'd found the portal to the god's hideaway and they weren't pleased. That wasn't worth considering. He moved his hands to her upper arms, lifting her from the bed with the pressure of them. That just made more of her ache and hurt. She moaned before she could stanch it.

"There is no tracking device in your suit."

Tracking device? Suit?

"Or anywhere else on your person. I checked."

He checked? That was odd. Wouldn't a god already know these things?

"Well?"

His voice was fading, but where he clenched was just painful and getting worse. She winced, and then got swallowed by the sensation of pillows again.

CHAPTER TWO

He had woman trouble. This was a first. Dominick studied the view of moonlight kissed waves from the master bedroom balcony. He didn't use this portion of the house. No one did. It was for show. This wing was always vacant and empty and he didn't care. But a villa on this chunk of coastline without a master bedroom suite - complete with a balcony - was bound to be looked at with curiosity, and that he did care about.

He rarely came up here at all, preferring the caves below. He'd carved large, impressive spaces into the rock before furnishing every single one as abundantly as anything above ground. Those corridors and rooms were his secret, and his alone. He'd personally designed each and every one for the solitude…and the dark. That's where he usually prowled.

But not tonight.

He had to get away from that woman. She was maddeningly incoherent and impossible to interrogate. Even now she slept heavily, without a care in the world, locked in the room containing his bed and still she slept…as if Dominick Miklos St.

Guis didn't even exist. That was just wrong. Dominick was used to females who swooned at a look from him; stumbled over their words if he spoke to them; dropped things, ran into things, gaped with wide eyes. They had for centuries now. The appeal was always there and he'd never questioned it.

Until this one.

Now he was forced to deal with a woman who not only ignored him, but added insult by slumbering the night hours away. All the night hours. Despite whispering and cajoling and threatening, and even holding her, placing his chilled flesh against her warmth, he hadn't gained more than a moan-infused breath or two from her; while he could have sworn each of her pulse beats were personally tempting him. He'd watched them thump along the line of her neck, her blood calling him to her as surely as he stood right here and right now.

Amazing. And totally unprecedented. Dominick had never run across the like. He'd also been wrong about her form. That woman possessed lush curves she wasn't amiss to shoving up against him, sending her very essence to seep out and linger along his senses, searching out and then toying with what had always been a solitary vampire, making him face the fact that women still did exist – and for more than a blood feast. She teased and tempted with every slipped breath, and then glazed her lips with a full flush of rose that had been more than this vampire could resist.

Dominick licked his lips now with the remembered taste of her mouth; tightened his knees against the odd weakness that afflicted them; clenched his fingers around the white painted iron of his railing. Every thought seemed filled with remembered contact with her. Every pore seemed tense and alert as if straining for more of it.

The Hunters had been very inventive when they'd hired and trained this woman. He'd need to alert Akron. But not until he broke her. It would be too humiliating, otherwise. Dominick didn't handle humiliation well. He remembered that from his prior life.

He turned from contemplation of the scenery, opened the slit of panel that hid his entrance, and started down the long spiral of steps that sucked one down into the bowels of his home. Despite the tight rein he put on his own body, his pace quickened the closer he got to her. The woman.

o0o

"You ready?"

He existed.

Oh sweet dream! She'd fallen into a real fantasy. Or something along that line. Courtney rubbed the sleep out of her eyes, scooted up against the headboard, and dared her eyes to again look toward where Apollo lounged halfway atop the bottom of the mattress, while the rest of him supported the position from the floor. It didn't look like a practiced pose but a sculptor would've had a field-day with the lock of black hair that tipped down right between his eyes, the frown putting slight furrows into his forehead, and his lips pursed in what was probably thought, but looked like a perfect kissing position. He seemed perfectly at ease, as if every day he sat with his arms folded and solemnity written all over that handsome face, while some naked woman lay spread in his bed for his delectation and enjoyment.

Wait a minute...naked? Where the hell was her wet-suit?

Courtney's eyes flew wide as she yanked solid fists-full of satin comforter to tuck with precision beneath her armpits. Then she assumed the exact same expression he was, although she was skipping the kissing portion. The bed was obviously well above the floor, it was canopied, designed with a flair toward Rococo if the amount of shell-work and cut-outs were to be believed, and it was massive. And private. And lit with a huge candelabra on her other side, shedding flickering light all through the enclosure. It was also quiet enough that when she swallowed, the popping sound in her ears was probably heard by him, too. That could explain the slight smile he gave before repeating himself.

"You ready?"

"What kind of open question is that?"

"You are not asking the questions here——."

"I know. I got that part already. But you take forever to ask any questions, and then when you do, it's an open-ended kind that could get you any answer. So, I just thought I'd jump in and assist. Do you have any food?"

He blinked rapidly. Eight or nine times. She lost count as the totality of his entire attention took her breath and then kept it from her. And her ribs were still hurting. That didn't make any sense. Not much about this did. She'd been deep-sea cave exploring, using Shawn's equipment. There'd been a large thumping noise, the shadow of a shark. She'd lost her air, then her consciousness. Somehow, she'd arrived in Mount Olympus with a Grecian god who'd forced her to drink some really excellent brandy. That seemed the total extent of her recollection. And nope. Nowhere in there had she hurt her ribs.

She probably needed to brush her teeth after the brandy and then napping hours away on this bed made of pillows. Courtney ran her tongue along her teeth and grimaced at the bacteria feel. She definitely needed to brush her teeth. She'd save that for after breakfast. Or brunch if she'd slept too long. Whatever this place provided, and whatever they called it, she'd be eating it.

"You know…food. Do they have room service here? Because I could really go for some breakfast. No wait. Coffee first. As black and thick as you can get it. Then food. Maybe some fried eggs, over-easy is my favorite. I'd like a couple pieces of toast with butter. And marmalade. I love that stuff. I could also manage a couple slices of bacon if they have it. What now?"

His expression had changed to complete blankness. He was still too gorgeous to continue to make words that weren't garbled together into gibberish. The man probably had a very good idea of his effect on women. That just made it worse.

"How did you find me?"

"I'm sorry. Courtney Dwyer. From Washington. The state, not the capital. Of the US. We were never formally introduced when I arrived at…wherever we are." She'd have put out a hand but that would release the comforter and that wasn't an option.

"Answer the question."

"What was it?"

He sighed. On that physique and with that countenance, it just created the exact same reaction with her, although she should have kept the slight appreciative note at the end of hers from being completely audible in the dead silence of the room.

"How did you find me?"

"I really hate to disappoint you, Apollo, but I didn't actually find anything. And certainly not you. Not that I wouldn't have been searching had I known how and in what direction you lay, but there you go. Hard to find something if you don't know it exists."

"What did you call me?"

"Apollo. I don't know your name, and that just seemed appropriate. Why? Isn't it right? Or are you Mars?"

He glanced heavenward for a moment before looking back at her. "Dominick. Dominick Miklos St. Guis."

"Strange. I had you pegged as Greek."

"I am."

"St. Guis is not a Greek name."

"It is from Normandy."

"Seriously? I should have known the accent was French. So…you're half French?"

"No. I am half Norman."

"Normandy is part of France last I heard. But ok. I'll play. I'm all for believing you don't claim French ancestry. I've never been to Normandy but I don't think the French are well-liked anywhere so I'm not surprised. Do they claim Scandinavian ties there? Don't look at me like that. It's painfully obvious. With your physique, what else could you be, but descended from Viking stock? The only other choice is Mount Olympus, and you pretty much vetoed that."

Stupid, Courtney. Her mouth just kept rattling off stupid things while her mind clouded with thoughts of intertwined limbs on the bed in front of her. For the life of her, she didn't know where the instant perfectly focused view came from. Worse, it looked like he'd been involved in every step of her thought process and imaginings, and that had just loosened her tongue more.

"My mother was full Greek."

"And she married a Norman. Imagine the potential lineage. Wow. Viking size and brawn mated to classic, perfect features. Stow that. No imagining necessary when the life-sized proof is sitting right there, looking at me." Courtney bit her tongue at the end of that, but it didn't prevent it from coming out exactly like that. Almost in homage.

"Who said anything about marriage?"

He skipped over the life-sized proof part. *Thank goodness.*

"Right. Marriage is optional. Always was, really. You know, I've heard children from love-matches are the most beautiful people on the planet. I'm not arguing that anymore. That's for certain."

Damn it! Her tongue just kept gushing inane words at him. He didn't even react to them. It was probably normal for him. Although…the more she spoke, the more his brow knit as he continued his unwavering look right at her. She started to amend that. It felt more like he looked all the way through her.

"Love was not involved. My mother was taken."

"Taken? Seriously?"

He nodded.

"How on earth could a Norman guy manage to get to Greece and *take* a Grecian woman? And why would he want to? Aren't there women in his part of the world?"

"My father was from the Norman settlement of Sicily."

"Norman settlement. Oh come on. There hasn't been anything like that for...I don't know. Eight hundred years or so."

He nodded. That was it. He just nodded. Then one eyebrow perked up slightly, and that little tiny thing sent her entire body into a shock-like motion of vibration. He might as well have tossed ice water all over her. If there was a hole big enough to sink into, she'd have done it. Right then and right there. And then, surprisingly, the entire view of coverlet started to rotate into a whirlpool of dark oblivion. It was perfect for losing herself in.

"Here."

He dented the mattress at her side, an arm behind her back to lean her forward, while a cut-glass crystal goblet was being held to her lips. She hadn't even seen him move. She took a swallow, gulped it, and then coughed with the reaction as brandy blazed its way down her throat again. That got her a smack of his hand on her back, and everything went into solid fire and agony.

"Oh, no. Stop. Please. Stop. You're hurting me."

She wailed it and he stopped. It still felt like he was bruising her just by the feel of his hand on her back.

"You did that before, didn't you?"

"What?"

"Hit me."

He shrugged, taking her with it. Heaven. Images of entwined naked limbs assailed her vision again and she blinked until it went away. She'd almost died, the god Apollo was holding her, he talked nonsensical heritage, she was in pain from his ministrations to save her, and she couldn't seem to prevent erotic images from filling her mind? He probably knew the last part, too.

"You needed air."

"I needed…air?" She still did. There didn't seem to be any room to get it from how he held her right against most of his body, while he'd changed the motion of his hand to a caress all along her spine. That was absolutely delicious. He probably knew that, as well.

CHAPTER THREE

It wasn't going well. It wasn't going much of anywhere.

Dominick looked out over the same view and wondered where his ability to interrogate had gone. He wasn't above torture. Never had been. Even if his target was a woman. Yet, with that siren sleeping now in the master bed that nobody ever used, Dominick was worse than putty in her hands. He didn't know what was wrong with him and he really needed to ponder it. He rubbed at the slight bit of scar on his upper abdomen, evidencing her attack. Another hour or so, it would be gone completely. A finger-span higher and he'd have been eliminated.

He turned to look through the diaphanous drapery rippling slightly in the breeze. The woman was in his bed. Asleep. Naked, and slightly tanned all over, and plastered against his form as he'd carried her swiftly right to this room. All she did was sleep. Touching her had zapped some strange sort of current clear through every pore on Dominick's frame and yet she experienced nothing. He'd been in a fury of motion to get her out of his arms before he acted on what could only be labeled lust, and what happened? The woman slept.

And worse.

He hadn't been able to simply place her between his sheets. He'd had to join her, rub against her, and groan with annoyance over his own body's reaction. He hadn't been able to stay his teeth from elongating, either, nor the hum of vibration as he sliced the slightest scratch all along perfect throat skin. He'd barely managed to rein in the incalculable desire to feed from her. Somewhere in his mind something worked, putting such a leash on him he'd jerked back...right from the precipice of fluid he knew would be ambrosia. And what happened? She'd slept through all of it. She'd even been doing some sort of purring noise.

Dominick blinked on the lightening sky that heralded an awakening for every other creature and the end of his. He had some thinking to do. Planning. Plotting. This woman was some sort of new weapon. She'd been infused with some chemical that over-rode every restraint he clamped into place, making it impossible to keep his mind on anything other than pleasure. While absolutely nothing happened to her. What sort of new device were the Hunters using? And how could Dominick subvert it? He'd spend some time on research before seeking her out again. That might work. For every potion, there was an antidote. He'd just have to find it.

But first he needed rest. And she needed sustenance. Dominick walked through the room, determined not to look at the girl. He made it to the door before failing. His own body was turning against him now? Whatever those bastards had invented, it was strong. Fast-acting. Long-lasting. Stimulating. Sense-awakening. All consuming. Overwhelming. Intense. He actually took a step toward her before the howl of frustration left his lips. Then he was in the hall and facing the white wood double doors that slammed shut against each other with his abrupt closure of them.

"You called, Excellency?"

Dominick turned. His servant bowed, dipping his turban with the motion.

"We have a guest, Rashid."

"Very good, Excellency."

"She'll be requiring breakfast. Or something of that nature. When she wakes." Dominick stopped his own words. He was a recluse for a reason. He never explained himself to anyone and he didn't understand why he had to start now. It was the woman and her potion. It had to be.

The man nodded.

"She's not to leave the villa. I'll hold you responsible if she does."

The man's eyes shone, but nothing else changed; exactly as Dominick required in his servants. Lack of curiosity and instant obedience.

"I understand, Excellency. It shall be as you require."

The man bowed again and left. And that's when Dominick remembered his secret panel was in the room he'd just left. *Blasted woman!*

oOo

Oh...heaven truly was luxurious! Courtney arched her back and stretched, feeling vaguely sore in her back, while satin sheets smelling of sunshine slid against her skin. Rays of the same daylight were percolating through an open patio door, giving her such a feeling of well-being the events of last night just had to be a nightmare. All except for that Dominick/Apollo fellow. Now…he was definitely not a nightmare. More like a really erotic dream.

"Good day, Miss."

Courtney's eyes flew open and she yanked on the covers to sit, staring at the strange man bowing from beyond the footboard of her bed. There was a man in her room. Her *bed*room. She glanced about, taking in acres of white flooring, an enormous white marble fireplace, French doors that opened to nothing but seascape, scattered, super-plush white rugs, and dark mahogany furniture that broke up the space. This was not her room. She was in another super king-sized bed. With another canopy. And still no clothes.

"Will you be taking breakfast now?"

"Where…am I?" Courtney's voice came out a croak, and for some strange reason, it hurt to use her throat.

"Villa St. Guis."

"Villa St. Guis."

He nodded and beamed a smile at her.

"Why…am I here?" And why did her throat hurt so? She didn't remember one thing about her neck. Her chest and lungs, yes. Choking and being forced to drink mind-numbing brandy, yes. Her neck? No.

"You are a guest of His Excellency, Prince St. Guis."

"Prince? The guy's a *prince*?" Courtney didn't believe it. No way. Not even in her inventive mind had she seen that coming.

"Had the Turk invasion not occurred, he would still be king, as is his birth-right."

"Turk invasion...as in...what? The Ottoman Empire thing?"

Courtney knew she should have paid more attention in class, but who could've guessed she'd need a brush-up on Mediterranean history now? The turbaned fellow nodded again and smiled, revealing perfectly spaced, white teeth. Against his dark skin, it was especially brilliant. Which was just special. The entire episode was growing into the special range. It was obvious to her now. Her brother-in-law, Shawn Elliot, was playing a truly elaborate prank. That's what he did for a living. He'd never tried it on her before. He set up scenarios, filmed them with his crew, and then posted the resultant footage on the net, making more money than her sister, Stella, could spend in this lifetime.

Shawn Elliott hadn't exploded into a million bits last night. Courtney hadn't been rescued and then beaten back to life by an absolute god of a man, and no way did she believe he was a king/prince. It was all a set-up. For Shawn. She was going to kill him when she found him.

"So tell me...where is my host?"

"Prince St. Guis is resting."

"Resting. Right."

The guy was probably working out in the gym, toning up that perfect physique, and doing a bit of lounging around on a pool deck chair before they sent him to make-up. She didn't know where Shawn found an actor capable of portraying a Greek god, but she was definitely finding out. She was also playing along until then. Starting now.

"What's your name?" She asked it and swallowed. Her neck hurt on the motion. She ignored it. She had bigger problems.

"Rashid."

"You know Rashid, breakfast does sound especially wonderful. I like my eggs fried, over-easy…some toast and marmalade, and stow that. I think I'll take pancakes instead. A double-stack. With lots of butter and syrup. And coffee."

"Do you take cream and sugar?"

"I'm about ready to take brandy again."

"You wish brandy? There is a decanter here."

He walked across the large span of flooring to show her several cut crystal decanters on what looked to be a silver tray. The mini-bar arrangement was on a high white shelf over near the patio window. Courtney set her lips. *Fair enough, Shawn. You wretch.* The servants weren't in on it. Or they were especially good. They couldn't even spot sarcasm.

"Coffee, Rashid. Black. And…where is my wetsuit?"

"I do not understand."

"I was wearing a black wet-suit. Beneath that was a fairly expensive one-piece fit especially to me. You know. Stuff like that."

"You were not wearing anything like that."

No lie. She wasn't wearing anything like anything. She was naked. As in…completely, bare-assed naked. Satin sheets felt especially decadent and sensual against naked skin now that she thought of it. Banish that! She had a vacant-faced servant looking across the room at her and revenge to plan. She didn't have time to enjoy any of this.

"Can I get something to wear?"

"There is an entire closet to choose from. Right here."

What the man called a closet looked like expensive white paneling, with the slightest dent in it that turned into a lever. Gossamer fabrics in all shades filtered out from the space once he opened it. They'd put together an entire wardrobe of dresses. Tons of them from the looks of it. Elaborate. And almost funny. If she didn't have to cross that span without a stitch on. In view of a hidden camera or two.

"Could you bring me a robe or something, Rashid?"

"You have a preference to color, Miss?"

"Courtney. Please. My name is Courtney."

"As you wish, Miss Courtney. Your preference?"

"Just make sure it's large. And concealing. And—." Her belly rumbled, interrupting her, and making Rashid pause at the closet with the volume of it. "Just grab anything, ok?" Her neck was really starting to ache. That was odd. Courtney reached to massage it and couldn't prevent the cry of surprise at the evidence of blood on her fingertips when she finished.

Blood?

"You have hurt yourself. Here. I have a cloth. I'll return shortly with your repast."

Rashid was at the table beside her bed, placing a white washcloth that was going to get stained atop a mass of purple-hued fabric. She didn't ask where he'd gotten it and he didn't offer. She didn't truly want to know.

CHAPTER FOUR

She should've been more specific. Courtney pushed that into her memory for later use. Don't ask a man to bring you a concealing anything. They have strange ideas on what that means. She might as well be naked with the sheer purple thing Rashid had provided. Not that it mattered. She'd already been in that condition – and unconscious at the time - and if that image was already on the web, Shawn Elliot was getting sued and Courtney Dwyer was changing her identity with the money. That's what was happening with that.

Men! That's why the top four listings on her Jerk List were men.

Courtney had created a mental Jerk List back when Stella was all she had as a relative and a guardian. Her sister was heartless, conniving, a great actress, and beautiful enough to stop traffic. She successfully pulled off being thirty, when she'd passed that mark eight years ago. Courtney didn't care. She had a thick enough shell around her to keep from caring about anything or anybody: bullies, teachers, counselors, Stella. But then her sister had married Elliot. Ugh. That man held the top position on the Jerk List ever since.

This servant, Rashid, was already on the list and he was in danger of rising. The man portrayed helpfulness, and gave the complete opposite. It was a waste of time to ask him for anything useful…like a phone. Or a laptop. Or even the front door. She'd had less luck with the three women she'd come across, painstakingly dusting and polishing every inch of what was already a spotless villa. No one understood her or they were being paid too well to pretend as much. Of course, with their attire, they could be Turkish for all she knew. She could even be closer to Turkey than Greece out here, and wouldn't know the difference. That's what came of worrying more about the right time to ask Shawn Elliot for a loan than where he was taking her.

Surprisingly, despite everything, she'd never felt better, but she'd never admit it.

It started with the breakfast selection and just got better from there. The coffee was robust and hot, her eggs perfectly cooked and seasoned. She'd even managed to eat a whole pancake before admitting defeat. The moment her tray disappeared she'd hunted down a bathroom, and got another surprise when she found it. That room was the size of her entire apartment in Seattle. The shower was a work of art fashioned into a circle of etched glass. There was a sunken pool that probably went for a tub, but Courtney wasn't a bath person…and it probably fit two. That just got her images of naked entwined limbs she banished the moment they surfaced. She'd *never* been one for erotic fantasies, and if she had to start now, it was not going into Shawn's little video.

Floor-to-ceiling mirrors came in helpful when evaluating the state of her injuries. That was odd. She should be a mass of bruising, black and blue from waist to shoulders…but no. The slightest touch of shading evidenced where she'd been man-handled. She had a long, wicked-looking scratch on her neck, though. It wouldn't stop bleeding. A bit of salve from the well-stocked medicine cabinet helped with the sting, and if she had to replace the bandage more than once, well…all-in-all, it was still too close to perfect to grumble much.

The view from this balcony had been spectacular before the sun set, too. Not that she felt cheated now. Each little lamp Rashid lit before bidding her good eve gave off its own little oasis of light. Why…even the stuffing in her chair was perfect. The flute of champagne she swirled in her hand added to the effect, and quite frankly, the entire thing was divine. She'd have to give Shawn that much. He had a fantastic eye for set-up and the bank account to pay for it. No wonder Stella hated him.

Courtney took another sip of champagne and sighed. Her time was about up. Soon that god-man was going to be with her again, mesmerizing her with the complete attention he insisted on giving her from bottomless black eyes, while tying her tongue into knots with the impact of looking at him while she tried to talk. It had to be her imagination. No man was handsome enough to scramble a woman's wits. It wasn't feasible and it wasn't happening, and that was that.

"You are rested?"

"Cripes!"

Courtney swiveled in her deck chair, wrapping the white dress she wore into a cocoon about her lower legs. She'd been wrong. This man was stunning enough to do anything he wanted with a woman. Any woman. Not just her. And that thought wasn't at all comforting.

"Must you sneak up on people?"

He ignored her for the most part, just as he ignored the chair on the other side of her little table. He must have known leaning against the rail and giving her a perfect look at his profile would be devastating. And damn it all, it was. Courtney took another sip of her drink before placing the glass with precision on the table top.

"I do not sneak. I entered. You do not listen."

"Haven't you ever heard of a contraction?"

He turned to face her, leaning backwards now, and that just put all that man in perfect line-of sight. Tonight he was wearing khakis and a black shirt of some t-shirt material that molded to eye-catching pecs before trying to cover up some truly amazing abs, and then it meandered somewhere beneath his belt-line in defeat. He wore his hair longer than she liked, but with it pulled back in a tail, it wasn't an issue.

What was she thinking? Nothing would look bad on this guy. And it wasn't her issue.

"You have forgotten."

"Forgotten what?"

"I ask the questions."

"Listen Handsome. You keep saying that, and then you muddle your way through some words, and nothing ever gets asked."

"Dominick. My name is Dominick."

It sounded like he was speaking through gritted teeth. On him, that was thrilling in a dangerous/sexy kind of way. It also made a river of goose-bumps rise on every bit of her skin. The man was solid sex appeal. Solid. She sighed heavily and dramatically.

"All right. Fine. You win. Dominick. But I rather like Handsome. I mean, surely you've been called that before. Somebody in your acting career had to have mentioned how drop-dead gorgeous you are. It can't be just me."

And why couldn't she just shut up?

"Acting career?"

"It's a stretch, but I suppose you could be a model. No. That'd be a severe waste. There's a huge chunk of folks looking for smoldering sexuality and man! Have you got the market cornered on that one. I'm the target audience of advertisers, you know, and trust me. You've got what it takes, although you'd probably melt the film every time they try to shoot you."

"Shoot me? Who else will try?"

He was closer, leaning down onto the table and making it groan with the weight of holding him. She hadn't seen the movement. The champagne flute wasn't the only casualty, as it rolled off the edge of the table and shattered on impact. It felt like her heart was going to come right through her chest. She had to wait several full beats and swallow before trying to make sensible words again.

"Wow. Here I was speaking of supreme sexual attraction, and you go and demonstrate. You've definitely got it, Dominick-my-man. In spades."

He narrowed his eyes next. Like that would do anything other than make him more virile and amazing. The man was over-acting, and he was good. Better than any day-time soap star she'd ever seen.

"Who else will try to shoot me?"

"Damn near everyone, I assume."

"What?"

"I said – damn near everyone who sees you will try—."

"I heard you!"

"Then why on earth are you asking?"

He didn't look like he got frustrated often, if that's what his howl exhibited. That, and the way he lifted the table from the floor, rippling major arm muscle before flinging it right over the balcony. That was just too much machismo. The table wasn't light. And he was being ridiculous. They'd probably make a fortune off this video.

It also eliminated any kind of barrier between them, and the next moment he was squatting at her side and looking at her with the darkest, sexiest eyes she'd ever seen. His position also made every thread of his trousers mold to every bit of muscled thighs and calves. And that t-shirt might as well give up the ghost. It didn't do more than cling and define. She couldn't help it. She sighed in full feminine appreciation.

For some reason, it looked like two small spots of color tipped the tops of his cheeks. That was totally unnecessary and overly done. If she'd thought him gorgeous before, she'd just been trumped.

"I will repeat this once more. I ask the questions."

She nodded, swallowed, and touched the bandage on her neck. For some reason, the sensation of heat radiated right through the gauze and into her fingers. He looked like he knew it.

"How did you find me?"

Courtney narrowed her eyes until he was blurred through her eyelashes. It helped. Not much, but it did help. She might even be able to get her voice to work again, especially if he was going to use broken-record psychology on her. That ploy was so see-through, it was impossible not to spot it. He was obviously being paid well to get this kind of action/reaction for Shawn's little e-film. That table into the sea stunt was probably going to get him a raise. Fine. She'd go with her original plan then. *Men!* Sometimes they were just...idiots. She pulled in a deep breath.

"All right. You got me. I'll tell the truth. We got word you were here. That's how I found you."

"From where?"

She couldn't keep a straight face long enough to get through this, but she was going to try. "Top source. Top." She repeated it soundlessly for effect.

"Who?"

Wow. He just looked good enough to kiss with his lips in that pout. She really needed to concentrate here. Courtney said the first name off the top of her head. "Kevin."

He frowned. On him, that was even stunning. "Who?"

"It's an acronym."

"A what?"

"It stands for... Kelp Evaluators...uh... International." She choked back the laugh but it wasn't easy.

"How?"

"How...what?"

"I ask the questions!"

"You are impossible! I can't answer if you don't tell me what you need the answer to."

"How did you find me?"

That was definitely said right through gritted teeth. A nerve poked out one side of his jaw, too, delineating it for her. Courtney gulped.

"It's a secret."

"You will tell me, and you will speak of it now."

Courtney regarded him for a moment. "Fine. You're onto me. I had a sending unit with me."

"There was no transmitter in your attire. I know. I went through it."

"You went...through it? My diving suit?"

"And the other thing you wore."

"What?"

"That is yet another question. I have warned you. I will not do so again."

"That other thing happened to be a four hundred dollar bathing suit! Four hundred, hard-earned dollars. You better not have damaged it."

"It has been shredded."

Courtney screeched. She kept her lips sealed so it wouldn't be ear-drum splitting, but it was still loud and angry, and it made her neck wound go to a solid throb. Nothing changed on Mister Perfect, though.

Not one iota of his expression. And that was just too much on an already wretched scene.

"I hope you're being paid a lot, Mister Dominick Miklos St. Whatever. And I mean a lot. Because I'm taking every penny. You hear me? And not just from you. I'm taking yours, too, Mister Elliot!" She'd looked over his shoulder to shout that part to the entire room before looking back at her host's enigmatic expression. "I am not amused. Not anymore. I mean, I wasn't amused before, but now I'm really—!"

Apollo/Dominick reached over and put two fingers against her lips, stopping her tirade in midstream with a solid jolt of sensation clear to her toes. And back. Courtney's eyes went huge, probably mirroring the look of shock coming from him.

CHAPTER FIVE

He shouldn't have touched her. He shouldn't be anywhere near her. Realization hit as the oddest roiling motion altered the elements about him. He didn't know what to say or do. She wasn't just a new weapon of some kind. She was something else. Something so huge, he didn't think he had the ability to grasp it at the moment. This woman awakened something massive within him. Fully. Indefatigably. Completely. Shifting him completely off his axis. The closest match he had was an earthquake.

Dominick had experienced enough of those. He'd had to rebuild the villa more than once, the last following the great quake of 1953. That one destroyed most of this wing as well as the kitchens. It hadn't the effect of this thing.

"What…just happened?"

The whisper touched his fingers, sending a tremor through him. All the way through him. Dominick blinked. It couldn't be. It wasn't possible.

He didn't subscribe to the theory of mating. He'd heard of it, every vampire did. Scoffed at it. There was no such thing as a person slated as his one true mate. The one being capable of making him whole. Fusing with him. Bonding with him. Making this entire immortal existence an eternity of pleasure rather than a constant repetition of nothingness. Such a thing was too fantastic to exist outside of fairytales. He didn't believe it, and he refused to start now. Not to him. Not now.

And not...*her*.

Dominick moved his hand, cradling it about her neck in order to lift her right to his nose, ignoring each whiff of air on his face as he narrowed his eyes and studied every facet of this woman. She wasn't exceptional. Nothing to take a second look over. She kept her honey-colored hair at shoulder-length, shorter than his. Light brown lashes encircled greenish-shaded eyes that stared wide-eyed at him. A light sprinkling of freckles crossed her nose. There was that perfect mouth, though, shaped for kissing. And there was a definite smell about her. Something indefinable that whispered of longings and needs he'd thought long lost and forgotten.

Dominick tilted his head, inhaling perfect woman scent as something shuddered into existence in the depth of his chest, radiating through every dead cell. Everything male in him responded. It wasn't an earthquake. It was solid, amazing, perfect, unmitigated wonder. If he believed in deities, he'd set out offerings, pen volumes of psalms, commit sacrifices in honor. Instead he went to his feet, melding her to him with his free arm. Then he went higher, hovering above the marble floor with the overwhelming volume of emotion he was trying to deal with. He couldn't stop any of it.

His spirit was soaring. Physical movement was simply a manifestation of it.

"This is not a good idea, Dominick."

She might be saying it, but the way her body stayed pinned to his, the quickness of each breath, and the swift lick she'd made on her bottom lip, plumping it even more for him, weren't demonstrating anything like it. The aura wrapped about them seemed to radiate from within. He'd never felt so light. His head was spinning with it and then his body joined in.

"You can just stop right there, Mister. I mean, no. This is so not happening. And you can just set me down, too."

If she hadn't been panting through it, cursing him with more perfect breaths, and if he wasn't hovering in a plane of existence that defied physics…well, maybe he could do what she requested. Maybe.

"You need to say something. I can't carry on a complete one-sided conversation. I mean, I can, and usually do, but I'm usually alone, too."

Say something? If he tried, it might be a sob. Emotion of this level and this magnitude was beyond his experience. His spinning slowed, widening to access the available space. If he still had a soul, it was singing. Something was filling his ears with orchestral sound.

"Listen, Dominick. No way did you get paid to do this. Even in Shawn Elliot's Pranks-Gone-Wild reality shows, there has to be some semblance of reality. Know what I mean? Who's going to believe you go from over-bearing asshole with one sentence lines to a lover with superman powers who…flies?

Did you put something in my drink? Because that's patently unfair. It's cheating. And you can add that to your video, Shawn-You-Jerk! How the heck did we get this high?"

She'd turned her head to yell something into the air about him, before becoming a quivering mass of female that latched onto him, her legs encircling his upper thighs while her arms looped around his torso. That was too much contact. Dominick fell, slamming to the floor beside his panel door, and the next moment he had her within the enclave of his sanctuary. To a vampire, it was easy to see and easier to navigate. To the woman in his arms, it must be terrifying. Pitch black and quiet, unless one listened carefully and fully while holding their breath. Then the slightest sound of lapping waves could be heard from his grotto, eighty feet below.

That could be what she was doing, since she'd decided to cease breathing. She wasn't controlling her heart-rate. That muscle was pumping her life fluid with rapidity, making her infinitely more desirable. Dominick hovered in the center of his rotunda, working to control urges and cravings that hadn't much hope of containment. He'd never dealt with such massive need. His arms tightened, and then trembled, and then went to all-out shudder as she struggled for control.

He was losing.

She called to him with every continued moment of their existence, and he hadn't any weapon to fight it. He couldn't. The denied feeding last night was a factor, but he didn't need fluid every night. He could go weeks without feeding. He couldn't go much longer without her. Everything on him knew it.

Stone stairs were carved into the sides of the rotunda. Two turns took him to each level and each complete arrangement of living quarters. Seven stories in all. As if he'd need the rooms. Carved wooden banisters encased the steps. He'd embossed silver atop the railing. It caught any light, looking like a fine-tipped pen had been put to use if he looked down. He didn't. The stair angle wasn't steep, nor was the spiral. Eighty feet separated the dimensions between where they were and the bottom step. He'd designed it that way on purpose. For efficiency, aesthetics, and speed.

Dominick ignored the steps to swoop down, the ascent causing strands of her hair to slide across his face where they caressed. Faster. Swifter. He was at the ledge leading to the fourth floor. The next instant, he was through the arch and within his rooms, where no living or dead thing had ever been, other than him.

The bed was another canopy, settled dead center in his room, elevated on a pedestal, as were all his beds. The maroon and black color scheme of his bedding nicely set off the dark Spanish oak construction. He placed her on his mattress, leaving her long enough to illuminate everything he could find. He didn't need the light source, but he was about to mate – with *her* - and he wanted to see every little nuance of it. He'd have been quicker but trembling gave him trouble. He couldn't even light a candle? Dominick looked at his own fingers in surprise after his third failure to keep a match lit.

"Ok, Dominick. Listen. I'm going to just pretend that little episode didn't happen. I am not here in some secret cavern with you, well away from any hidden cameras and sound feeds. I did not just go flying through the air, drop like a rock, and then end up in yet another massive bed. No. Didn't happen. And I am not in a setting resembling something from a Victorian stag film. Not that I've ever seen one, but I've heard of them, and I have a fairly decent imagination. I mean, it must be decent...and then some. Look at what I'm imagining here. Oh my. I mean, oh frickin' *my*."

Her words ended with a garbled sound. Dominick didn't ask why. He'd leaned across her to set the candelabra on the headboard, using both hands so nothing would rattle. The headboard was crafted thick so it could support the width and weight of so much silver and candle wax. It was also high. Golden glow flickered about as it embraced the interior. Dominick didn't wait to evaluate it. He didn't dare. His fingers were giving him trouble again, and he needed to unlatch the semi-sheer panels of his canopy to pull them into place, creating an oasis of privacy. She started talking again as he reached the second post at the footboard, stopping him momentarily.

"You need to say something here, Dominick. I mean, really. I'm not exactly immune to this plan of yours. Damn it. Why does my mouth always have to trip me up?"

He slipped a glance at her then away. It was the best he could manage.

"Or at least ask. You're transparent as all get-out. Anyone can see through this. And it's not like

I'd truly turn you down. What am I saying? Does any woman ever turn you down? Ever?"

Turn him down? He puzzled that before letting it go. It had been too many centuries since he'd needed a woman. There wasn't much asking. What a man wanted, he took. Women were then left to fester with hate over it. His mother drummed that into him before he'd even reached puberty.

"I mean, I admit it. You're the most gorgeous man I've ever seen. You've got the body of a god, the face of a model, and the heat coming off you is enough to melt asphalt. You probably have the package to back all that up. Geez. I should just shut up when I'm ahead. I wouldn't even mind the 'I ask the questions' stuff right now. Trouble is...now that I'm ready, you don't say a word. Not one. I mean, I'm all for the strong silent type, but you're taking it to the extreme. And I do mean extreme."

She'd interspersed her words with a low tone when she'd mimicked him. He almost smiled, but caught it before exhibiting elongated canines that were sure to startle her.

"You probably should've been warned that when I get nervous, I start talking non-stop, and then I sound like a complete idiot. As if you can't figure that out for yourself. Shawn probably counted on it. Except...I'm pretty sure he doesn't know where we just disappeared to, and how. Damn it! I'm not discussing how we got here, because I'm just not. It probably looked very good on the web, though. How did you do that anyway? Did we really just fly? And no. Don't answer that."

One panel had a knot in the tie attaching it to his foot post. Dominick pondered it.

"Um...I'm really nervous here and that means I'm talking. And you're not doing anything to help the situation. Nothing. In fact, you're making it worse. Oh, don't look at me like that. You already know exactly what you do and in what measure. It's probably practiced. I get it. You're not just an actor, you're an athlete. That explains everything. Women probably swarm all around you. All the time. You don't have to sweet-talk them. It's a waste of time. So. What sport are you in? Soccer?"

He didn't answer, and she must have told the truth about her verbosity because she just filled in the gap with more words.

"Fine. Don't answer. I'll figure it out anyway. Can't be soccer. They don't have your height and bulk. That would slow them down. Swimmer, then? You don't have to tell me. I'll nail it sooner or later. I'm really good at this. It's what I do. I facilitate communication. We need that in today's web-driven world. That's what I went to Shawn Elliot for. His money. I needed a guarantor for the bank loan. You don't think I'd be with him for the pleasure of his company, do you? I've got it. You're a dancer with a mean sense of rhythm and—."

"Warrior."

If the lifted eyebrows and open lips were an indication, he'd surprised her. Dominick watched where she sat, her words momentarily halted. Then something changed. Her face took on a blank look as she regarded him silently. It didn't last.

"Warrior? Oh, please. Let's just pretend that occupation didn't disappear with what? The Trojan Wars? Roman conquests? Oh! I get it. You're a

Special Forces kind of dude. That's what you mean. And you can just stop there."

His fingers froze on the knotted tie while he looked across at her.

"What? I'm supposed to be too stupid to notice you're setting up a seduction here? Give me a break. No. Give me two of them. Come on, Dominick, say something else. I'm really feeling awkward and nervous over here. And I just told you that keeps me talking. I'm called 'motor-mouth' for a reason. Heaven knows what will happen if I get scared."

He yanked the drapery tie apart, making the entire bed structure creak. He regarded her through the sheer curtain, blurring the view. She did look a bit scared, with wide eyes, hair that haloed her head, while both hands were clasped at her breast.

She didn't know what she asked. If he made any sound, it would contain the raw primitive emotion he was suffering. If she felt nervous now, she'd be in allover fright. He didn't dare speak. So he kept his steady regard on her, fully and completely. He moved out an arm and lifted the drape, lowered his chin, and called on his skill to mesmerize and enthrall; concentrated to bring on the humming sensation that hypnotized and froze his prey...and got nothing.

Dominick blinked on the proof before his eyes. He should have known his power wouldn't work. For centuries now, he'd been able to wield it. But not now. And not with her. If anything, it looked to have the opposite effect. He watched as she sucked her bottom lip into her mouth and started breathing shallowly and quickly. The panel could just stay where it was.

The next moment he was at her side, rocking the mattress with the force of his entry as he gathered her into his arms.

CHAPTER SIX

Her words halted, and every thought behind them. He had her pressed against him, held in the curve of his body, while the most amazing vibration emanated from where her nose pressed, right beneath his chin. It spread from there until it encompassed her entire frame, sending her against him in a continual set of surges she hadn't any control over. Or maybe it was his movements engendering the same response. It was incredible. Stirring. Sending myriad images in lightning progression through her mind, all of them featuring naked, entwined limbs. On this bed.

Nothing could have prepared her. Especially for what happened next.

He put a finger beneath her chin, using it to tip her face to his, slanting his head down slightly at that same time. She wasn't given any choice save to look right into his shadow-enhanced gaze. The result was breath-stealing. Heart-stopping. Enough to stop time and make it cry defeat. Courtney was ensnared. She couldn't blink. She couldn't move. She couldn't think. She didn't know if she'd be able to take her next breath. Dominick had beautiful eyes of darkest brown. Deep, and bottomless, and sending her senses into overdrive. A flicker happened, coming from the depth of black she stared into. It was snuffed the moment it happened. The resultant shockwave jolting her entire frame wasn't as easily extinguished. Or endured. And since there wasn't a particle of air space between them, there wasn't any way to hide it.

Except to open her mouth and say something. Anything. Before she dove right into the pit of sensual ecstasy his look promised.

Words didn't happen. Dominick lifted her, the same moment he dipped his head, and took her lips, restarting her heart with such a kick of fury, it pained. Heat infused her, ratcheting everything to an even higher level. There was a long drawn-out moan happening and he stole it with a kiss that weakened not just her knees, but every muscle in her body.

He didn't give her any time to assimilate any of it before shimmying his body upward slightly, sliding hard male against her, bowing about her, enclosing and protecting...and possessing. He moved the kiss to her chin, gaining a murmur from her, as he licked his way along her jaw-line. A thigh curled up, splitting her legs beneath it, while his hands moved to cradle her shoulder blades, lifting her without expending one ounce of effort. Courtney's head lolled back, gifting her blessed space for air, as he slid his tongue to where the bandage should have been protecting her scratch.

His body arched more and his fingers tightened, gripping fabric that hadn't any prayer of staying whole, and then solid absolute pain hit her right in the throat. Agony raced through every portion of her, chased there by each pulse beat. Courtney stiffened in shock and surprise. Every bit of her choked cry carried it. And then something changed. Stings of sensation erupted, spurting outward from where he sucked at her neck, blurring the pain into a riot of wanton, lustful, overwhelming need. She was soaring. Thrilling.

Courtney's eyes slammed shut while her mouth stretched wide to let the longest, throat-tearing cry out.

"Agapimeni."

Movement accompanied the gruffly whispered word, unlatching him from her neck to trail the kiss back to her lips. What felt like a razor sliced along her inner lip, paining to such a minor degree, it didn't rate worry. There wasn't any time before the pleasure hit again. Sweet heaven! Her body arched in reflex, planting her right against him. This time she was more than soaring. She was flying. And this time, her senses erupted with such amazing ecstasy, her entire being reveled in it.

She was lowered back to the mattress, still gulping solid enchantment from his lips as he did hers. He settled atop her, accommodating his bulk between her split legs, and she wrapped those about him, clamping to linen-covered hips and thighs to rub all along hardness his trousers didn't do anything to mitigate. His other hand meandered from where her neck was throbbing with remembered bliss, down her arm, taking her clothing with it. Then he was above her, in a push-up that just put masculine perfection in perfect view. That black t-shirt thing was useless as covering once a light source got behind it. It was see-through. What a waste of clothing.

This guy should be forced to walk about shirtless. Her hands moved to mold around his pecs, supporting him while he studied her. The entire time he wasn't breathing. He wasn't blinking. He wasn't doing anything other than focusing entirely on her while her heart sent every beat with force. Then he dipped his head, touched a kiss to her nose, and actually said something.

"I am asking."

She was going to swoon. Literally. That had to be what the rush of ice-cold sensation portended, before it was followed by heat, and all of it chased with goose bumps that flew everywhere.

"Asking?"

Her whisper didn't make sound, but it didn't matter. He sent a look to where her hips straddled him, imprinting shivers without even touching.

"Yes. Asking. And now…I am waiting."

His loins pulsed at her and then one side of his mouth lifted in a slight smile. Courtney felt her heart swoop with another physics-defying move to pound from her lower belly, where it joined the throb of need and lust and passion already there.

"You need it…in words?" She panted through the disconnected words. "Please say…you're joking. Come on, Dominick. Really."

He grinned, revealing the sheen of blood-red hued liquid as well as really sharp spikes. That just wasn't possible. Or real. Or anything other than such over-kill, it was laughable. Shawn Elliot truly expected her to believe this guy was a vampire now? It was exactly what he'd need for his prank.

Laughably, so. Her body couldn't seem to find that reaction however, as Dominick lunged upward, unlatching her legs to yank off his shirt and toss it somewhere behind him.

Wow!

Courtney's mind went blank on a view of masculine perfection that came close to strangling her with the sucked-in breath. It seemed to create a like reaction in him, and now the open mouth exhibited fangs that looked even longer than before. Her heart wasn't just reacting; it was attempting a leap right out of her breast. She clamped both hands there as he shoved backward to the floor, unhooked his pants and dropped them, without releasing her unblinking gaze. Not once.

Her jaw dropped fully, especially as he stretched, as if preening for her gaze. The guy was strutting now? Was she that obvious?

Of course you are, Courtney. She tried to tell herself any woman would be, and shoved that thought aside the instant it surfaced. He wasn't with any woman. He was with her. The guy was perfect, he was definitely locked, loaded and ready, and she was the woman here. And if he wanted her to believe he was some sort of vampire, it was fine with her. She didn't care. Not one bit.

"You did say yes?" He tipped his head slightly.

She gulped, nodded, and then he leapt atop her. The bed rocked in submission, her gown had the same issue as he literally pulled it apart down the front, and her entire form wasn't far behind. Courtney's mouth latched onto his, devouring the kiss with a fervor born of need. Passion. Absolute craze. She was drowning without one drop of water involved.

Harsh breath filled the enclave. Her lip split and she tasted blood…evaluated, and then reveled in it. Her fingers flew over his back, the fingernails sliding against flesh. Her legs wrapped about him, holding him to her, the position matching her earlier erotic vision. All of her pulsed toward him in an endless series of lunges. Desiring. Striving. Demanding. And wherever she touched sent sparks.

He moved the kiss down her chin and to her throat, feeling like it opened flesh, and then he latched onto her again, sucking and licking and sending nothing of pain, and everything of ecstasy. Courtney rocketed with it, the canopy above her rotated before wide eyes, and then descended into raging red-colored want. Need. Hunger. The emotions pounded through her; rampant, base, overwhelming.

His hands were hard, commanding, gripping to her hips to hold her pinned in position for his entry. It was Courtney who lunged up to join them, embracing and enwrapping, and taking everything he was, over and over, in an increasing volley of give and take. His hair had come loose, dropping strands of it to join hers, mingling dark and light about them.

There was no control. There was only joining. The mattress rocked beneath them, assisting the wild movements. Heat built as fire-like flickers consumed the area. Throbbing pressure built, along with heart pounding, breath stealing need. Light infused the entire area and it didn't emanate from any candle. She tried to clamp her eyes shut to all of it, but then such beauty hit, her eyes flew wide on everything. She was in a bow of absolute wonder, her mouth stretched to accommodate the cry as everything careened into a time-consuming vortex of ecstasy.

The keen died away, absorbed into the deeply-voiced grunts that accompanied Dominick's movements. Muscles bunched and retracted, his face scrunched in concentration, pumping in an ever-increasing motion that just kept building. Harder. Faster. Another spark ignited, flared, grew, and consumed, sending her into another realm of amazement, accompanied by another harsh, throat-tearing cry. And again.

The man was a machine. A wonder. A complete mystery. Where Courtney gripped, she slipped; her arms, legs and entire frame alternately tightening and then going limp, and still he filled her, giving absolute pleasure, and total satisfaction, and then it changed. Dominick turned into a churning monster of motion, shoving into her with hard thrusts that kept rhythm with the deep grunts that accompanied them, and then he moved his head, speared her with a dark look that completely stole her heart, and dropped his head.

This kiss stole. And it stunned. And then it warped, changing her entire reality as he went ram-rod stiff, his loins pulsing against her as he emptied into her. He shook, moving her with it. She wasn't just tasting life fluid; she was slavering in it, sucking and licking, and for the first time in her life Courtney knew absolute and complete fulfillment. His movements slowed, stilled, and then he sank into the embrace she'd kept on him the entire time.

His weight was crippling but she wouldn't change a thing. One hand lazily stroked at his lower back, and then his buttocks, following hills and valleys of skin-covered sculpture. Wow. She'd never felt like this. Ever.

And then a loud alarm thing went off, making them both jump.

CHAPTER SEVEN

"Looks like I'm interrupting."

Amusement colored the words. Dominick didn't move his eyes from a screen that showed a shadowed desk fronting a stone fireplace. Nothing more.

"I'd apologize but that's just not my style. Aside from which, you've been ignoring my messages. I only use the alarm when I need to."

"State your business. I am busy," Dom finally replied.

"Wrong answer, St. Guis."

Dominick pulled his hair back and circled the tail with a band, taking his time. Waiting. Then he smoothed down his shirt. Wonderful material. Didn't wrinkle. The same couldn't be said of his pants. Definite crease marks showed where they'd lain crumpled on the floor. For what hadn't felt like hours, but must have been. He didn't take his eyes off the screen the entire time.

"What do you wish of me?" he finally asked.

"What? No pleasantries? No inquiries to my health?"

"I pity the fool who worries over your health, Akron."

"Hmm. You? Pity anyone? Never. You want to tell me what happened?"

Dominick pursed his lips and waited. Such a question had too many answers, all of them meant to entrap. It was Akron's usual method. And Dominick didn't waste words if he didn't have to.

"You want me to fill in the gaps?"

"You are the one calling this meeting."

"I've got a problem. It deals with you. And that means, you've got a problem. Me."

Dom nodded and waited again. Akron finally sighed.

"It's about a little thing called media attention. I avoid it at all costs. I thought we were in accord about it."

"We are."

"Well, we've got a lot of it now. Messages circling the globe. Speculation. Investigation. Inquiry. Rampant publicity. A soon-to-be-recognized widow who is very annoyed and not leery of texting over it. Using her toss-away, untraceable cell-phone to my unlisted and now vacated number. Silly woman. Everything leaves traces and I don't give refunds."

"You have woman troubles?"

"We're not discussing me."

Dominick grunted a reply.

"There's been a vessel lost at sea. A rather large yacht belonging to a fairly prominent and wealthy man. Happened during a pleasure cruise. Disappeared without a trace sometime last night."

"So?"

"The search is on. They're using all resources. Military. Civilian. Mercenaries. All sorts of riff-raff looking for an opportunity to cash in on the publicity...*Hunters*."

Dom stiffened without meaning to.

"Taking a kill this close to your home was a risk. Taking the entire crew was even more so."

"It was an accident. I was not responsible."

"You take an assignment. It gets screwed up. You're responsible. Got it?"

Dom nodded.

"This gives me a very nice conundrum. I now have to waste time watching as they widen their search. Perhaps close in on your secrets...and that could lead to mine."

"They will never find me."

"You fulfill the contract?"

"Yes."

"How many involved?"

"Six. No. Five."

There was a chuckle at his slip. Dominick's hand clenched. He didn't let it be seen.

"You want to elaborate on that loose end?"

"I do not have a loose end."

"You really should try putting contractions in your speech sometimes. You sound archaic, along with foreign. Both very identifiable features. Romantic. Considering you're already very memorable when seen in person, it's too much."

"I am never seen."

"Keep it that way. There's not a woman around who wouldn't remember you to a finite degree. Probably most men, too."

Dominick flushed. He could feel it. "Your point?"

"You were paid well for this assignment."

"I am always paid well."

"Four-point-three-million. In full."

"So?"

"So...I'm in a quandary here, Your Highness. I need to decide whether to launch an offensive against your island or not. There's sensitive information that could get leaked. This means I have to take a chance and I don't gamble. You're not giving me enough information to make a decision. Perhaps you could find some communication skills and start talking."

Dom sighed. "I found her, Akron."

"Who?"

"My *mate*." His voice slipped on the word, revealing too much. He couldn't help it. He still couldn't believe it.

A long whistle sounded. "You sure?"

Dom leaned back in his chair as if considering an answer. Or the stupidity behind it. "Yes."

"This is a definite complication. She's from the yacht?"

"Yes."

"Hmm...reported missing is internet sensation Shawn Elliot, his personal secretary, three crewmen, and a rather uninteresting figure listed as Courtney Dwyer. That her?"

Dominick nodded.

"She see anything? Know anything?"

"Not yet."

"Hmm. I see. I'll keep in touch. Don't ignore my messages again. Oh, and Dom?"

Dominick stopped with his finger on the power switch.

"I wouldn't tell her you just killed her brother-in-law. Or that her sister paid for it. Never mind."

"What?" Dom's forehead wrinkled in a frown.

"She's standing behind you. Catch her before she faints, will you?"

The screen went black.

CHAPTER EIGHT

Shock was an undervalued condition, especially the numb part that seemed to accompany it. Courtney was solidly in its grasp as she rounded the fourth circle of steps in her quest to get out. Her heart pumped madly and she panted from the exertion, but that was better than dealing with what she'd just heard and was expected to believe. No. Wasn't true. Didn't happen. Couldn't be. Nothing like this happened in the world anymore. Well…maybe on some new cable show, but not to her. People from Seattle didn't end up in some Mediterranean labyrinth; they didn't have their world blown to smithereens about them; they didn't wake up with millionaire princes; they wouldn't fall heavily into passion-drenched lovemaking sessions with them; and they'd never be expected to believe that said wonder-guy was a real-life murderer.

It was bad enough he had vampire delusions and acted on them. No. That didn't happen either. None of this did. Courtney blinked against a blurred view that smeared the steps into one long snake built of stone. She wasn't just denying this entire episode. She refused to believe it. Period.

Numbness should've gotten her to the top of this damn spiral staircase. She should be racing steps, rather than watching the series of them distort, elongating before her eyes. There was a landing of sorts where the steps semi-vanished into what was probably another floor of his cave mansion. She'd passed three of them. Maybe four. The guy must have ten floors in here. That wasn't fair.

Fair? What a joke.

She blinked, clearing her vision again, and then she was at the next set of steps. Hearing that self-confirmed asshole, Shawn Elliot, was dead didn't bother her. Much. He had such an over-inflated vision of himself, the world all of a sudden felt bigger. Her sister using his own money to rid the world of him – now that bore consideration, if and when Courtney got past the bigger one: She'd actually bedded the murderer...and loved every moment of it.

Argh.

Numb was supposed to last longer. Courtney swiped at both cheeks. She wasn't facing any of it yet. She had time. She had to get this physically grueling climb behind her first, though. It was obvious Apollo/Dominick didn't need to work out much. All he had to do was climb his stinking stairs.

The man loomed out of the shadowed recess marking the next floor, making her stumble. Courtney grabbed for the rail, wrapped both hands around it, and looked over the precipice at darkness that went a long way down. The steps were safer. She turned back. But that meant she had to face him...and everything that went along with that.

The split dress she'd tied back together with one of his canopy ties was sweat-damp at her waist. She supposed that helped keep it closed. She didn't have a stitch on beneath it, and silk skimmed and stuck to just about everywhere. She was sticky with sweat. Her heart was pounding so hard she could barely hear her raspy breaths over it. Those breaths were close to taking her to her knees with the strength of them. And that god/man didn't even look winded. He just looked good. All-over good. She sneered up at him.

"You could…have told me…you had…an elevator." The words were broken into sections controlled by her panting.

"I do not."

"You don't." She corrected.

"Yes," he replied.

"Oh stop already, Dominick Miklos…St. Guis. If that is even…your real name."

"Why would it not be?"

He raised one eyebrow as he asked it, putting way too much emphasis on how gorgeous he was. Her tongue felt swollen. She needed to look at something else. She settled on the cavernous black behind him.

"Why wouldn't…it be," she repeated finally.

"That is what I said."

It was getting easier to breathe. If she kept the conversation littered with trifles, and avoided looking at him, her heartbeat might ease up as well. It was worth a try.

"I heard you. I'm trying…to demonstrate…how it should be said."

He pulled back and stood to his full height, which was considerable, thanks to that Norman heritage. Then he crossed his arms, putting massive arm size atop ripped abs on display. There was that Norman stuff again, added to by a warrior work-out he probably did. He had one side of his face scrunched in thought. That just highlighted the Greek ancestry. Damn everything, but the guy was stunning, even in that configuration. Courtney nearly sighed aloud with it.

She really needed to look at something else.

"You are correcting me?"

She nodded.

"I do not find it necessary."

"You don't."

"Exactly."

Subtlety wasn't working. She should've known. Men must have little use for subtle. She was going to have to give him the "it's been fun, but we're finished" spiel in words. Courtney inhaled and exhaled four more times, deliberately holding each before sending the air back out. By the final one, her heart felt almost normal.

"Look Dominick. I'm leaving. It's been…interesting. No…more like—."

"You cannot leave."

"Yes I can. And will."

"It is daylight."

"So?"

"I cannot go out in daylight."

Figures. The guy was still working the vampire angle. She should use it to her advantage…and could start now. "Well I don't have that problem. So, how about we just say goodbye here?"

"I do not say good-bye."

"*Adieu?*"

He shook his head slowly. Cripes, but the man was stunning. Dense, but stunning. She'd have to give him that, again, and move on.

"*Adios*, then."

"No."

"Well...I don't know how you say good-bye in Greek."

"You do not."

Courtney gave the resultant frustrated sound through her teeth and slid around him. She moved exactly two steps before he was blocking her again. She hadn't even seen him move.

"I need to get out, Dominick. I need air. Fresh air."

"You cannot go outside. It is unsafe."

"Oh, come on. Stop with the vampire stuff."

"Stuff?"

"The sunlight burning the skin stuff. The immortal, blood-drinking stuff. You know...stuff."

"You know of vampires?"

"Who doesn't? Now, let me pass."

"It is not safe."

"Oh, for the love of—. Fine. We'll play, then. You're convinced you're a vampire? Ok. Believe it. No skin off my nose. I've heard worse. Watched programs. There are lots of people specializing in delusions of all sorts of things. Including vampires. I, for one, don't happen to believe in them, and I'm pretty sure I wasn't turned into one last night. I wasn't...was I?"

She actually looked to him for confirmation. That was stupid. She held her breath awaiting his answer, and that was even more stupid. He finally shook his head. Courtney felt her shoulders relax. She'd been worried? She really needed fresh air!

"That being the case, I can still go outside. Sunlight doesn't hold the vaguest fear for me. I won't even get sunburned since I spent weeks going to the tanning salon to work up this tan. So...you may not be able to go outside, but I sure as hell can."

She moved to go around him. He blocked her again and that was just going to get him all kinds of argument. Somebody should have warned him about that, too.

"I cannot allow you to leave. It is not safe."

"You want to try the 'broken record' thing again? Fine. Two can play this, too, Buddy."

"Buddy?" he repeated.

"You keep saying it's unsafe and I'll keep repeating my answer, as well. It's perfectly safe for me. I'm not a vampire."

"But, it truly is not safe."

"I can go anywhere. I am not a vampire."

"You may not have heard. There are Hunters about."

"Hunters." It wasn't a question. It was too absurd to even mouth it.

He nodded.

"What, pray tell, is a Hunter doing in the middle of the Aegean Sea?"

"They are everywhere."

"Hunting what? Vampires?"

He nodded.

"And...just how do you recognize a Hunter? Do they wear camo?"

"Camo?"

"Or…maybe hunter orange is more their style. They wouldn't want to shoot each other by mistake, now would they?"

"They give off a smell."

"A smell." No matter what she said, he was just as dense and she was just as stuck. "Get out of my way, Dominick. I'm warning you."

He stepped to one side. Courtney took a second to believe it before stomping her way around another complete spiral in the steps. He met her at the next level, blocking it with about two hundred fifty pounds of man…claiming to be a vampire. That was ridiculous. Vampires didn't grow to two-hundred and fifty pounds. Unless they were at that size when they became immortal and it never changed. Or…maybe it did change, and they had to consume tons of calories. Blood didn't have that many calories. Or maybe it did. How the devil was she supposed to know? It had never been listed on her weight-control chart. But cannibals had always looked pretty skinny in pictures. Maybe that's because they had to exist on jungle forage in the meantime.

Shock did weird things to conscious thought, too, she decided, looking over all that man. Despite any exertion, he still wasn't breathing hard, and here she was, with a stitch hitting her side. She didn't care how much he weighed or however he maintained the poundage, it was enough to block her exit. She crossed her arms over her heaving chest and looked up at him.

"How did you get up here?"

He sucked in on a cheek and avoided meeting her eyes; both signs of an upcoming lie. Great, Courtney. Just great.

"I...ran?"

She was in trouble if he resorted to lifting that brow again. He was well aware of it, too.

"You probably flew again. Tell the truth."

"You would not mind?"

"I *wouldn't* mind," she corrected.

"Truly?"

"Of course I'd mind! I'm correcting your formal, nonsensical pattern of speech, here. It's the least I can do before getting the hell away from you and then I'm going to fall apart. Is that all right with you?"

"I do not find my speech a problem."

"No shit, Sherlock."

It was either the content or her tone, but he went from being slightly mussed, affable, and nonchalant, to immediate bristling, virile, and terrifying. If he had a weapon, she'd be facing it. The dropped chin and narrowed eyes were inflicting more than fear. *Shit.* She'd forgotten. The man was a possible murderer, she was hidden away in some cave with him while the entire world thought she'd vanished, and he was playing at being a blood-sucking vampire, and doing a darn fine job of it.

Courtney's throat went dust dry and her heart decided to change rhythm, thumping with a two-part maneuver somewhere in her chest. Tap-wham! Tap-wham! Tap-wham!

"I do not appreciate your words."

She licked her lips. He snarled, revealing very wicked-looking fangs that looked pretty real. Then he lunged forward backing her right into the railing that bit into her tailbone.

"Were you not my mate, you would be dead."

Dead.

Mate?

Tap-WHAM!

That pulse thump really hurt. Courtney put both hands to her breast to prevent her heart from slamming its way right out of its enclosure. There was a spark in the depths of his eyes again, and it didn't just flicker away. It was deep red in color…a glowing deep red. She could've sworn it contained heat, too. But that was ridiculous. Everything was. There was reality in here somewhere. She needed to find it.

CHAPTER NINE

"You rang?"

Dominick looked at the shadowed desk and wall showing in his screen. He'd sent the message hours ago. It wasn't worth mentioning. "I need another assignment."

"The girl?"

"I need to know about a society."

"This is why you need an assignment?"

Dominick shook his head. "Kelp Evaluators International. KEVIN for short. I cannot locate it in an internet search."

"That's because there's no such thing."

"There has to be. She said she works for them."

"Well, she obviously lies. You see, this is why I stay out of complications like mating. It's a severe waste of time and manpower. Just look what it's doing to you."

"What?"

"Sit, St. Guis, and stop prowling. You should change your clothing, too."

"My clothing?"

"You're insufferably perfect in dress and manners. Always have been. Insufferably. But look.

If my eyes don't deceive me, you've got creases in your trousers, your shirt on backwards, and tell me that isn't one sock with your shoes. In fact, you almost look human for a change. Mating must really agree with you, lucky dog. You should have requested it sooner."

"This is not luck. It is the opposite. And I did not request this. I did not even see it coming."

A heavy sigh came over the speaker. "Nobody ever does. Sit."

Dom slammed his palms to the table instead and snarled into the laptop screen. "The assignment, Akron?"

"Anything in particular?"

"Massive."

"As in…?"

"Lots of force required. Physical. Nothing hidden. I have a need to hit something. I need you to fulfill it."

"I'd heard true love's a road littered with potholes. You seem to be a perfect example."

"You amuse yourself at my expense?"

"Apologies, Your Highness. It's too great an opportunity to miss. I've known you for centuries and it's a pleasure watching your unwavering aristocratic shell develop cracks. A supreme pleasure."

Dominick shoved away from the table and backed to a far wall to glare at the monitor from there. "You have an assignment or not?"

"I always have assignments. I'm just debating how to respond. You're rather hot property at the moment – beyond the normal."

"Hot property?"

"Covert is your style, Dominick. Exposure is not. Anywhere I place you I have to consider the fallout should you get seen."

"I am never seen."

"Taking a cute little number like your mate to an assignment will make that a bit difficult, don't you think?"

"She is not going."

"On the contrary, she is definitely going. Staying anywhere near your villa at the moment is impossible."

"The Hunters?"

"They make the authorities look like amateurs. They've deployed deep-ocean sonar subs and I have to respond. I'm sending a 4D team as we speak. I'm rather glad you made this call. Otherwise, I'd be interrupting your little love tryst with news of your impending evacuation. Both of you."

"You will destroy the villa?"

"Only the caves. Destroying that prime chunk of real estate aboveground brings unnecessary complication, and I've already got enough of that at the moment. Speaking of…where is your little mate?"

"She is locked in one of my rooms."

"How positively barbaric."

"It is her own fault. She would not cease heaping recriminations at me. At ear-blistering level."

"No wonder you want to kill someone. She's probably hatching plots against you as we speak."

"I have her on monitor. She is sleeping."

"Better and better. I almost wish I could accompany you to Colorado."

"Colorado?"

"In the United States. Four corners Colorado. Coyote area. You wanted a massive assignment, didn't you?"

Dominick nodded and approached the screen again.

"There's a cult over there. Normally off the radar. Just a little group of fifty or so. They don't take well to their members leaving. Seems a young lady tried just that. They found some of her body two days ago. Coyotes are great scavengers but didn't take care of all the evidence. That young lady's father has a lot of money and a lot of anger. And now he wants revenge. Anyone with a weapon he wants eliminated. He's offering two million a head. You interested?"

Dom smiled.

"Leonard will be your contact. He has all the details. Oh. And Dominick?"

"Yes?"

"You shouldn't have tied her to the bed. That was overkill. She's going to be very angry when she wakes. Just warning you."

"How did you—?"

"Monitors are easy feeds to tap. And I'm an expert. You may want to remember that in future."

The screen went black before Dominick shoved it off the table, making it a permanent condition.

oOo

The smell of scented candle wax woke her. It accompanied the slide of liquid silk nearly everywhere she touched. Courtney yawned and stretched and toyed with keeping her eyes closed. She could almost be back in Elliot's yacht, except the man didn't go for putting anything except premium-grade Egyptian cotton sheets on his beds. And then her toe touched what could only be a bare man's leg.

In her bed.

Courtney yanked back her limb with the same swish of movement that had her sitting, holding bedding to her breasts, which just uncovered more of him. He had a penchant for large beds and enormous candelabra. Neither one was doing her equilibrium any good. She narrowed her eyes on her nemesis, Dominick Miklos St. Guis. It didn't do a thing to mute how stunning he still was. Too bad it hid his true nature: Perfidious. Dangerous. Lying, scheming, cantankerous…male macho jackass.

Considering she'd just placed him at the top of her enemy list, and added a possible epitaph to boot, he took it fairly well. All he did was lean back and put both hands to his hair, pulling it away from his face as he pillowed his head. Courtney forced her eyes to stay glued to his face, focusing on his perfect sculpted jaw. It wasn't helping, but if she concentrated on finding just one slight flaw, maybe she'd staunch how the rest of her suffered rampant tingling.

"Good eve."

"There's nothing good about it."

"No?"

"You're here. In my bed. Without permission as far as I can recall."

"You seek to wound with words, but your eyes tempt with heat. Both speak volumes to me about…permission."

He sat, pooling the errant bedding into his lap, so it could form a base for showcasing perfectly formed chest. The man was more than stunning. He knew it. And he knew she realized it. Her sigh was just icing on the cake to him.

"You appreciate what you see, *Agapimeni*?"

"What does that mean?"

"You like asking questions."

"Come on, Dominick. We're way past the 'I ask the questions' phase of our relationship. Beside which, you never ask any. And you didn't answer. So, I'm asking again. What does *Agapimeni* mean?"

He smiled, showing pearly teeth without one glimpse of fangs. It was devastating. The bastard.

"What?" Courtney asked.

"You have titled this a relationship. I approve."

"It's not up to you to approve or disapprove. And you're avoiding answering. So, I'm going to do the broken record thing. What does that word mean?"

"It means 'my love.'"

Oh…no! She gulped. Her heart thudded into over-drive and that was just shy of giving her a head-ache. She narrowed her eyes. "I wonder why that sounds not only unlikely, but presumptuous as well?"

He leaned closer somehow, looming about her, while the immediate flare of candles helped with the impression. Courtney's gasp was loud. There wasn't any way to hide it. So she licked her lips and started talking.

"Come on, Your Highness. I admit it. I'm way over my head here. It's obvious you've got more experience than me. You've got a gilded tongue and looks to match. You probably entice women to your bed for the fun of it. Or the exercise."

"Do not use titles with me, *Agapimeni*. I am Dominick to you. Or if you prefer...Dom."

"You see? There you go again."

He lifted one eyebrow. The result was worse than devastating this time.

"You didn't answer my question," she informed him.

"There is a question asked? When?"

She licked her lips again. It didn't help much, but it gave her a little time to try to curb the nervousness that was going to become words she couldn't take back. And then she just asked it. "How did you get so experienced?"

"Experienced?"

"Yeah. Experienced. As in pleasuring women. And don't go and say you don't know what I'm asking. I refuse to believe it. You're experienced, and that means there's a powerful amount of women involved. That could lead to complications involving health organizations. I'd like to know now if I need to worry."

Courtney sat there and felt every bit of the blush infusing her as she waited for him to deny it. Putting a number to prowess was the last thing a man admitted. If a woman asked, they deserved the lie they got. Instead he gave her a huge grin, reached for her, and enfolded her into massive arms, resting her cheek against his chest. The bedding hadn't made the move with her. She ignored it. She really didn't need or want it. Skin on skin was too heady an experience, while she felt cocooned in warmth.

A fingertip touched her chin, lifting her to face him. She locked gazes with him. Any hint of

amusement was gone. The spark of red was back
deep in his eyes, drawing her into a vortex of red.
And black. And sending pore-raising electricity.

"I have little experience, *Agapimeni*, and it is so
far in the past I cannot even recall. The pleasure of
which you speak is due to who you are. What you
are. And how it is when we are together. Finally."

"We?"

"You are my mate. And I am yours."

"Don't do the vampire stuff again, Dom. Please?
I'm not certain—."

His kiss stopped the words, her heart, and her
ability to breathe. And then all of them slammed
back into existence. The resultant lunge against him
was impossible to hide. As was the frenzied attempt
to meld right into him. The man had the ability to
rob her of common sense, reality, and truth. But he
replaced it with an amalgamation of emotion,
sensation, and awareness. The room spun, re-
righted, and then spun the other way. Courtney
slammed her eyes shut.

"Do not deny me, please?"

The words accompanied the slide of his lips to
an ear and then to her throat, leaving a trail of wet-
kissed chill the entire way.

"Dominick...I—."

"I...love you."

Those three words, said with the barest quaver
through them, robbed her will and sent her spirits
soaring. Totally. Courtney's dismay evaporated,
spinning into the whirlpool of amazement that had
him at the core. A vista of wonder opened, even
behind her tightly closed eyelids. She barely felt
duel pin-pricks of pain at her neck. The resultant

uproar was absolute fire. It raced through her veins, sending passion laced with bliss, fervor coupled with wonder, and wanton need mixed with ecstasy.

"Oh Dominick! Yes!"

Her voice showcased the mix of sensations she dealt with. He didn't answer, but his sucking motion intensified, showing he'd heard her. She could've sworn they rose, soaring well above the mattress, while the entire room rotated about them. She slit her eyes open to watch.

Dominick's arm tightened and he went rigid, lifting his head despite her whimper in order to sniff, grab her to him, and move in a blink of time to a crouch beside the bed. And then the walls imploded.

CHAPTER TEN

"What's…happening?"

It wasn't possible to go from eroticism to panic without something giving it away. The squeak in her voice was an excellent example. Courtney swallowed on what was going to be full-tilt screaming as one moment they were beside the bed while Dominick wound them together in a sheet, and the next she was aloft and heading for a solid stone wall.

"Just a moment, Your Highness."

Dominick spun, taking Courtney with it, although her vision seemed to be behind the move. A lanky, black-clothed man stepped through the dust and rubble. There were more black-cloaked figures with him. Courtney froze with fear, contrasting all the more with how Dom seemed to relax. She didn't have time to ponder it before he addressed the tall guy as if they weren't facing annihilation.

"Findlay."

"It's *Doctor* Findlay to you. From D4 Team Blue. Akron sent us. We've got about…four minutes. Maybe five. You can even take the stairs."

"Good."

"Don't go up. It's blocked. There's a fairly large group of Hunters at your villa gate as we speak. If I set the charges right, I'm going to nail about eight of them. Easily. I'm very thorough. Don't leave much that's recognizable. This little cave of yours is about to become rubble. It's my new trademark."

He motioned about him with his machine gun thing. Courtney narrowed her eyes. It didn't look like any weapon she'd ever seen. That thing was more lethal.

"My jet is waiting."

"The jet is history, Pal. You going to move or am I going to have to shoot you first?"

Dominick stiffened. "You would not dare."

"True. But my wife won't hesitate. Sasha?"

Courtney stiffened as a stunning brunette stepped in to stand beside her husband. Even encased in something resembling a black wetsuit, she was stunning. And if Dominick had women like that about, why on earth would he look twice at Courtney Dwyer?

"Stop talking nonsense, Stuart, and see to the destruction phase. You'll have to forgive him, Dom, but he's a natural. He really takes to destruction. Blowing stuff up. General mayhem. It's his hobby anymore. You need to leave. Now. Use Domination."

"Don't tell him to do that," Courtney complained before she could stop herself. "He's an expert at it already."

The brunette pierced her with charcoal-hued eyes and then smiled. She directed her words to Dom, but didn't move her gaze from Courtney. "Dominick Miklos St. Guis. She's a baby."

A baby? Courtney was every bit of twenty-four. Jerks. They were all jerks. She was adding all of them to the list. If she had one of those weapon-things she'd knew where she'd be aiming it. She wasn't a VIDWAR marksman with over forty-two thousand registered kills for nothing. Another explosion rocked the ground.

"Time's ticking!" Doctor Findlay announced. "Move! All of you!"

"Hold to me."

The whisper hadn't reached her ear before Dom was moving. He didn't take the stairs. That might be too civilized. No. He flew full-tilt at the stone wall, swiveled just before impact and slammed his back into rock. Boulders and debris filled space that contained a lot of black nothingness and not one speck of floor. Courtney got a whiff of fresh air that changed to an acrid odor of something unpleasant burning. She wrinkled her nose, Dominick jumped into a complete freefall, and he should've been prepared for what happened.

She screamed. Long and loud and with every last bit of available breath. The shriek echoed about them as he landed, the thud jouncing her against him.

Her throat felt raw, and the place they ended in was so bright it hurt. Dominick didn't seem affected at all. Courtney blinked around moisture until it focused into an underground launching site, well-equipped and stocked with cranes, a railing loading system, lighting, and space to dock a cruise ship if he wished. Right now it looked conspicuously empty. There seemed to be quite a lot of crew about, among them Rashid. Courtney looked over the very correct servant, immaculate in white tunic and slacks, a turban still neatly wrapped about his head. He addressed Dominick and patently avoided noting her.

"Excellency?"

"Rashid."

"The motor craft is ready, per your orders."

"Good."

"Motor craft?" Courtney whispered.

As if in reply the water rippled, became the top of a slick, black, stingray-looking object, and a few moments later a prow appeared. He had a stealth-boat? She didn't know why she questioned the proof looming there, dripping water from its ascent. Courtney's eyes went wide and her jaw dropped. And she was getting really tired of having those reactions.

"My craft. I call her Domination."

"Of course you do. No wonder that woman called me a baby. She's probably still laughing. I'm not the least surprised, either."

"She would not dare."

"Oh yes, she would. That's why she said it."

"No. That was for me. She has no room for comment. Her mate is newly-turned as well."

"I'm not newly turned, and we've still got a lot of dialogue before we go into the 'mate' phase of this. Ok?"

"I do not know why you fight it so. There is no need. You are my mate, Courtney. She recognized it."

"Bull—."

Another explosion rocked the area, sending chunks of the cave roof into the water about them. Dominick held her to him, rocked with the motion, and ignored how the water splashed all about them. For some reason, Courtney felt completely safe the entire time.

"Quick. Use the ladder. We must leave. Right now."

"I'm not moving."

"It is not a request."

"You can't just pick me up and take me along whenever you feel like it. Not only is it inconsiderate, but it's not helping your 'I'm your mate' cause. Where – exactly – are we going, anyway?"

"Colorado."

"In a ship? I'm pretty sure Colorado is still a land-locked state."

"I have a jet in Athens."

"I don't know why I ask. I really don't. Of course he has a private jet, Courtney. He probably named it Intimidation."

He sighed in a supreme motion that moved her with it. She barely kept from giving one herself, except his was filled with exasperation, and hers would contain something more along the line of adoration. Damn him, anyway.

"You need to enter the watercraft. This is gaining us nothing. I cannot allow the Hunters to gain you. Please cease arguing and climb up."

"I'm beginning to think it's a gender thing."

"You still argue?"

"Men. They just can't see the obvious. I'm not moving without you. Period."

"I will be right behind you, *Agapimeni*—."

His voice quavered again. Courtney's heart dropped. Her eyes misted. All of it worse than wrong. *Stupid. Supremely, totally, overwhelmingly stupid.*

She didn't dare feel anything for him. She had her reasons. Not only was he way too pretty, but he'd be completely unmanageable. Prone to violent episodes. Able to bust through stone walls. Chuck heavy tables right into the ocean. Swoop and fly without expending an ounce of effort. He was being hunted. He had some very odd friends...and she might as well admit it.

He really was a vampire.

They might not exist, but that didn't change it. The guy was a true creature of the night. She didn't need a relationship therapist to see they'd never suit. Courtney forced every emotion away, aimed for the most sarcastic and cold tone she could, and actually thought she managed it.

"Whoa. Down, Boy. It's not what you think."

He blinked and looked like she'd hit him. That was just at her tone. Courtney kept it up.

"I'm not going anywhere without you because we are wrapped in the same sheet. I'm not about to prance about stark naked. Are you?"

"My name is not Boy. It is Dominick."

If she'd thought him dangerous before, she'd been mistaken. The look he gave her literally stopped her heart. He looked chiseled from marble and just as hard. His eyes weren't warm, nor were they glowing. They were black and obsidian cold. Death-cold.

Courtney couldn't control the shiver. She didn't need to be a vampire aficionado to read that look. If he didn't believe them mated, she'd be dead. History. Yet even now, with murderous intent covering him, he was still jaw-dropping gorgeous. Her mouth was bone dry and everything on her shook. He didn't say a word, only reached over his shoulder to pull the end of the sheet loose before stepping back from her. Then he wrapped the rest of it about her, rippling bared chest muscle the entire time.

And he had on thigh-length skin-tight black swim trunks.

"Go below. Rashid will escort you."

He jerked his head and another explosion rocked the chamber. The resultant chunk of stalactite barely missed spearing where Dom stood, ignoring everything as he kept his eyes on hers. She'd been right the first time. Domination wasn't the name of any stupid boat.

CHAPTER ELEVEN

He'd been mistaken. This mate of his was a remarkable woman. The more he was around her, the more amazing she grew. She'd be the perfect assassin: nothing to look at twice, and a complete mistake to overlook. It wasn't any individual feature; it was the combination of them. She was well-formed. He got a very good example of that since she'd slid her way into his embrace hours earlier and stayed there. She had those greenish eyes, blemish-free skin, perfect lips, and this ash-blond hair that easily curled. She hadn't dried it from her shower, taken after demolishing two burgers and a half pound of deep-fried potatoes, washed down with a couple of lagers. According to Rashid, she'd been humming to herself through most of it, too.

It wasn't just her physical features. Nor was it the wondrous smell wafting from every portion of her. Dominick lifted the lock of hair curled around his finger to his nose and sniffed, and that got him jolted by electricity only she seemed to have. The sparks she sent were more than considerable. They were addictive. She wielded it without any effort right at him. He blinked on a sudden wash, blurring her image, and then forced the rampant emotion down.

This mating thing was overwhelming at times.

"We really have to stop this, you know."

Her words lifted him from contemplation of his finger to meet her eyes. The moment it happened, he suffered a solid surge of primal arousal that sent his body into full rigidity. Dominick worked at controlling it, solidifying and tensing every muscle at his command, until it almost worked. He only hoped the moisture in his eyes wasn't noticeable.

She wasn't unaffected. Or the quick slip of her tongue to her lower lip didn't mean anything. Nor did the instant tremble of her entire body where it matched to his. Dominick tightened a bicep to lift her; thrilled at the contact, and then suffered another semi-seizure of reaction all the way through him.

"I mean...uh...every time we're together, the world is either exploding around us, or we're in bed."

Color touched the tops of her cheeks, her blush sending liquid fury racing through his veins, elongating his teeth and making him shudder with containing it.

Not yet.

"Together. Uh...without clothes. Again. It's a real...problem."

"I do not see the problem." His voice was lower, containing so much bass it reverberated through the chamber.

"Of course you don't. You're a guy. Sex and explosions is probably "Guy Heaven.""

"Guy Heaven." He repeated.

"Ok. We'll go slower. We need to communicate. As in...have a conversation. Do you think we can do that without adding explosions?"

Her breath was a curse of provocation, crippling him with every word as it slid across his chin, touched his chest, and then slithered inside to reach his heart. If he answered verbally, it might be a sob. He nodded.

"Good. Now...let's move on. Can we have some meaningful dialogue without sex mucking up the works?"

"I do not know."

The words shook and sounded sobbed. Dom bit down and got pooled blood in his lower lip from his own fangs. She gulped. He didn't see it or hear it, but as close as he held her, and as attuned as he was to every nuance of her, he easily felt it. That righted his world. Not completely, but enough.

"Well...at least you're honest."

The slight air from her words seemed to cut right through him. Everything on him reacted. He had her gripped in his arms, his legs about hers and worse. They were hovering above the mattress. If he remembered any appropriate curses, he'd have used them.

"This...is not working. And you need...to let me go."

She panted through the words. Dominick stopped the rotation that would have wound the sheet about them. Let her go? Never.

"I can't even think...when I'm this close to you. And we still need to have a talk. Now. Please?"

The plea filtered through somehow, worked its way through his senses and cooled what felt like raging flames. Dominick lowered back to the bed and loosened his limbs, and somehow kept from grabbing her back when she slithered away from him to the other side of the bed. She gathered her legs and a prodigious amount of bedding to her in order to sit, facing him.

"Good. This might work. No. I think you'll need to sit up, too. Come on, Dominick. It's not like you're a real Greek god, lying around, while you wait for a nymph or two to drop in."

Dom regarded her for another moment, and then sat. He ignored where the covers slid but could tell it truly bothered her. He watched her flick a glance to his lap and back, while a blush infused her cheeks. He sucked in on his cheeks and narrowed his eyes, and somehow kept the hunger at bay. Barely.

"Wow. I mean. Wow. This is so patently unfair. You should come with some sort of warning label or something."

He lifted an eyebrow and waited.

"Maybe we should get dressed first. It's hard to think of words."

She licked her lips again. He pulsed in place. And then she sighed audibly.

"I mean it's all well and good to hear of vampire stuff, but when it's in front of your face. Well. It's really different, you know?"

He waited a few moments while the sound of her words dispersed. He shook his head.

"They're very sexy. Vampires, I mean. What am I saying? You're very sexy. The vampire part just adds unnecessary mystique. I know. I'll just tack on your age. You're old. Way too old. Ancient, even.

What was that about the Norman stuff? That was about eight hundred years ago. Maybe nine hundred. Right?"

"I am twenty nine."

"Sure you are."

She looked as skeptical as she sounded.

"Exactly as I was when turned. I cannot recall a moment of the past centuries anymore. How can I? I've found my mate. You."

Hell and damnation. He'd put inflection on the words that made her eyes widen while her lips gapped for breath. Her breath. Sweet. Sending tendrils of lightning that sparked right into him.

"Dom?"

She had the plea sound in her voice again. It chained him without iron. He made such tight fists about the sheet it shredded between his fingers. He locked every facet of his body as he shuddered for control. When he looked back up, she was watching him with unblinking eyes and the slightest whiff of fear. That wasn't at all what he wanted. He wanted her fearless and challenging and spouting her words at him. And that finally worked at cooling urges and passions that no being should have to leash in.

"About…this mate thing."

"Yes?" The word trembled.

"I'm not so certain there is such a thing."

"There is."

"How do you know though? I mean, you've had close to a millennia of time. Surely there have been women—."

"Fate seals two as one. It has been this way since time began. You are my mate. It's fated."

"What if I think fate is just a by-word for weakness?"

"Weakness?"

The word angered. He added that to the emotions he held at bay. It probably sounded in his voice since she stiffened. That just added unnecessary ballast to the cravings since the sheet molded to feminine curves that were already making his world a misery of suffering.

"If things go wrong, it's fate. If things go right, it's fate. If you get cancer, it's fate. If you're healthy, it's fate. If you get rich, it's fate. If you end up homeless, it's fate. See what I mean? It's an easy thing to blame."

Dom regarded her for a span of time that could have engendered hours or mere moments. "I am not weak," he finally told her.

"Nobody ever said you were. Geez. Could you just put aside all the male macho nonsense and think here?"

"There is no thought involved. You are my mate. It is not optional. There is no choice."

"There's always a choice."

He shook his head.

"So…I'm just supposed to up and accept that you're claiming me and that's all there is to it? I don't get to say no?"

"You wish to tell me no?" The words were choked and guttural.

"Would you abide it?"

She didn't know what she asked! Dom hunched into a whorl of frustrated need, digging gouges into the mattress with holding it back, playing at a facade that didn't match one bit of it. She should be able to tell from the way the bed rattled.

"I do not know." He finally replied.

"Wow. I mean...wow. Dominick, listen. It's not as if we don't click, like...supremely well. It's amazing. Making love with you is...well. Uh. More than I can describe. I mean, I've never run across anything so patently male and sexy in my life. That's not it. It's just...we hardly know each other, and mating sounds a lot like domination, and that's just not me, and...um. Would I have to turn into a vampire, too?"

He was on his hands and knees, having arrived in a blink of time to hover above where she'd fallen back, her hands on his chest, propping him from contact with bent elbows and stiffened arms. It didn't work. His lips were on hers, pulling at her essence, sucking and tasting and drowning in the bliss, while his traitorous tongue spouted words he wasn't even hearing.

"Ah...*Agapameni*. You do not understand. I cannot hold it. It is too vast. Too...large. I love you. I cannot help it. I thirst for you. I need you."

"You're right. We can talk...later. Much later."

She mouthed the words along his neck, licking her way to a spot behind his ear. Dominick groaned in appreciation at the first flick of her tongue against his earlobe. And then he arched upward in supplication as she nipped at him. And then he lost all semblance of control. And took her with him.

CHAPTER TWELVE

Heat radiated off the tarmac in waves, alternately sucking life and moisture from every living thing that got to participate. Courtney shielded her eyes at the desolate section of dirt and scrub brush just off the asphalt. It felt like the cool cotton of her sleeveless top and shorts were already stuck to her and she hadn't even exited the plane yet.

"Wow. He didn't say we were going to hell."

"We are just outside Grand Junction, Colorado, Miss Courtney. It is not hell."

"Remind me one of these days to teach you about sarcasm, Rashid. I think you'd be a natural," she replied.

"As you wish, Miss."

Rashid waited at the bottom of the steps for her, a satchel in one hand and a purse in the other. He handed it to her once she joined him. It wasn't hers. It was part of Dominick's stash of female clothing and accessories, but it was nice to have a purse back, so she didn't quibble over it.

"Where is Dominick anyway?"

"His Excellency is resting. He cannot go out when the sun is up."

"That isn't a sun, Rashid. That is a fireball from hell. It's going to fry my eyes. Did we pack sunglasses?"

He set his satchel on the ground where it immediately gapped open, and without any searching, he found a pair and handed them to her. They looked military issue and unfeminine but they were dark. Rashid was a very efficient servant. No fun to talk to, but he was efficient.

"So tell me, Rashid-my-man, do we have some sort of transportation arranged?"

"Of course."

"And...you're going to tell me where it is?"

"We are early. It hasn't arrived yet."

"Then why are we off the plane? At least in there it's air conditioned, even if it still feels like I'm moving."

"We have a minute, thirty-seven seconds to the pick-up time."

"A minute, thirty-seven seconds. Rashid. You're fired."

"Of course, Miss."

"Are you always this pleasant? And cool? Sweat's already dripping off me and yet here you are, covered head-to-toe, and actually look refreshed. What's your secret?"

"I sleep when I have the chance. I do not have the luxury of playing video games when I should be resting."

"I can't sleep during flight. Never could. And I'll have you know I'm a Gray Class marksman in the VIDWAR system, with so many registered kills I have a hard time getting anyone to fight me."

"This is a good thing?"

"I'm an expert shot. With any weapon. I'm higher ranked than most of the West coast. And then some. If you knew your gaming systems, you wouldn't have to ask."

"I see."

His eyebrows lifted and she saw a shadow of a smile before he turned to watch a vehicle, getting discernibly more distinct through heat waves as it neared.

"Where are we staying anyway?"

"The prince has lodgings reserved near Bookend Cliffs. At a hotel belonging to a national hotel chain."

"A national hotel chain. A vampire is staying at the national chain hotel? Why am I finding this hard to believe?"

"We always stay in hotels of this nature."

"May I ask why?"

"Anything else could engender interest."

"A servant from the Middle East, wearing a turban, arriving in this desolate place on a private jet - and booking a coffin into a room - wouldn't already do that?"

"A coffin?"

"Of course. For Dominick to travel in."

"His Excellency does not travel in a coffin. Why would you think such a thing?"

"I was raised on vampire lore. Everybody thinks that."

"Well. It is wrong."

"So...how does he travel?"

"You should ask His Excellency that when he joins us. Come. Our transportation approaches."

"How long have you been with Dominick, anyway?"

"My entire life."

"You're a vampire, too?"

"Miss Courtney. Please. I am out in the sun."

The car was a tan SUV with tinted windows and black rims. It rolled to an easy stop right beside them. Rashid flashed a quick smile, showing teeth that would have blinded if she didn't have her sunglasses on. She put him higher on her Jerk List.

The man who stepped from the vehicle could have been anybody. Average height. Average build. Sandy-colored hair with a receding forehead. Khaki colored slacks, blue polo shirt. Anybody.

"Hey! Welcome to Four Corners! Don't bow, Rashid. This is the US of A. No obsequious greetings allowed. I'm Leonard. But you can call me Len. This her?"

He stuck out a hand. Courtney lifted her brows and looked across at him.

"Her who?" she asked with a cool tone. He dropped his hand.

"Why…St. Guis's mate. Was told to expect you. Welcome to the family. What? No bags?"

"I'm not his mate." Her grand cool attitude got ruined with a yawn.

"Right. Come along anyway, then. Looks like some sleep is in order. We've rooms at the hotel. With big soft mattresses and tons of air conditioning."

He winked and opened the back door, motioning her into cool, dark interior. She didn't know why she fought it. On second thought…

"Are you a vampire?" Man! She wished her mind worked on zero sleep.

"Not likely, Love. Look about. It's daylight. You know...you might want to be a little nicer to your sitter. I didn't exactly ask for the chore."

"My...sitter? As in *baby*-sitter?"

"Not unless you plan on acting like one. Get in. It's baking out here."

"I do not need a sitter. I'm perfectly capable of getting places myself, and I'm close enough to home to make a break for it. Why on earth would I get in?"

"St. Guis has my sympathies. And this is going to cost Akron double. Would you please get in now?"

She was close enough to reality to smell it! At the hotel she'd have more than air conditioning and a bed. She'd have a phone. Or she could stand out here and argue while turning into a sun-baked sweat-ball. Courtney got in.

oOo

"You rested?"

Courtney's nose came off the pillow and she blinked it into focus. She'd have moved her hands to swipe at her eyes, but the chains stopped her. Damn it. Damn it. Damn it.

"They put you in cuffs?"

"Dominick. Finally. You know...it's been uh...fun. I've had a wonderful time, really."

He pulled and one chain ripped right through the wooden post of her bed, allowing her to swivel onto her back. It was bad enough being chained to a bed without being in that position. She'd never felt so open and vulnerable, and—

Holy cow. Her jaw dropped and her heart was right behind it. The guy was worse than stunning. He was menace and threat, and shiver-inducing. She should be used to the sight of him by now. But dressed head-to-toe in black with two short swords strapped to his belt and the hilt of another rising from behind him, and there were no words. Seeing Dominick the first time had shocked and stunned. Seeing him dressed like a warrior in the VIDWAR game could be her undoing. Easily.

"You are not to be harmed. By anyone."

Len was really high on her Jerk List, especially since she'd almost made the lobby the second time he'd caught her. Now, she actually feared for him. "He...didn't hurt me. Look. They're padded."

Dominick hooked a finger beneath the metal and snapped it. He dispatched the other one the exact same way, leaning over her to do it, and then he looked down at her. She really should disguise some of the awed look she probably wore, and the slight smile on his lips showed he saw it. Evaluated it. And knew exactly what caused it.

And this guy *claimed* her? Amazing.

"Come. The moon has gone behind a cloud. It is time."

"Time to do what?"

"My contract."

"You're assassinating someone aren't you? Just like you did with Shawn."

"Shawn?"

He really didn't know his name? "Shawn Elliot. My former Brother-in-Law, Shawn. From the yacht."

"Oh. Him."

"Yes. Him."

"In that event, no," he finally replied.

"So…you're not going to go and kill someone? Then what? You're attending ComiCon?"

"I am not going to kill anyone like I killed Shawn. That was a failure and I do not fail."

"He's dead, isn't he?"

"Along with several innocents. Come. We're wasting time."

"Shawn was an innocent."

"He was a businessman with a bent toward crime. He had a contract out for his wife, Stella. She had a contract out for him. She contacted the better firm. Us."

"Please don't tell me my sister is dead."

"No. I believe she is in the Witness Protection Program at the moment."

"For what?"

"Safety. She is still the target of a contract that has yet to be filled." He held out his hand.

"Stella? Look, I know she's heartless, but really. This is a lot to swallow."

"Tomorrow. We can speak more of this tomorrow. For now, hold to me."

"How can I contact her?"

"You? You are counted among those killed in the explosion of the yacht. Your obituary was very short."

"You're joking."

"I never joke. Now, come. Please?"

"I can walk."

"We are not walking."

"This should be good. What are we doing, then?"

She didn't need to ask. It was a good thing it was dark and he didn't go very high. At the speed he moved, it wasn't more than a blink or so later before he seemed to just stop, descend, and then crouch, taking her with him. His hold wasn't needed. Courtney was glued to him with both arms and legs. She untangled them from him and smoothed her shirt down over her waistband before rubbing at her arms. She was under-dressed for being out in night desert air. It was chilly.

"Where are we?"

She whispered it, which was stupid. They were in the middle of nowhere, atop a rock precipice, overlooking a large span of desert valley. And then she noticed a small circle of lights marking some sort of settlement.

"About time you got here." Len's voice preceded the desert-camo clothed man, crawling toward them.

"How many?" Dominick asked.

"Eight on the perimeter fence. Six inside. They secure all their cult members in the underground complex for the night. I understand this is a ritual for their faith. I think it's more like prison."

"Weapons?"

"Automatics. Side-arms. Extra clips. Grenade launcher at the front gate. No info on the inside. Sorry."

"What is that?" Courtney pointed.

"Cult devoted to peace – if you can believe that. Trouble is they don't exactly practice what they preach. They kill anyone who tries to leave and they're too stupid to keep from leaving evidence that a rich father can find and then seek vengeance for. Which explains why we're out here…if you take my drift."

"You talk too much," Dominick interrupted.

"Right." Len whispered back.

"You stay here. With Courtney."

"You're taking on fourteen plus armed men by yourself?"

"I wanted a large assignment."

"I'm supposed to sit up here baby-sitting your little mate again? No way. And if you're sentencing me to that, you really should anticipate the argument."

"I am to have her with me. Akron's orders. I will not have her harmed. By anyone. Including you."

"Look. If she wasn't such a wild-cat, I wouldn't have cuffed her. But come on, St. Guis, I used my sex cuffs. They're fur-lined. Nothing drastic."

"I will take that up with you later. When I return."

"Dominick?" Courtney reached and put a hand on his shoulder. He might have been looking at her, but she couldn't tell. "I have a really bad feeling about this."

"*Agapimeni*. This is child's play. Wait. Watch if you like. You have the glasses?"

"Please. Do I look like the beginner here?" Len replied.

A pair of binoculars was placed on the ground beside here. And then Dom was gone. Just like that. She didn't even feel him move from beneath her. All she felt was rocks and sand.

CHAPTER THIRTEEN

"It's taking too long. I can't see anything."

"It's been five minutes since you last said that. And you never see anything if St. Guis is involved. The man's practically a shadow. I'd think his mate would know that."

"You're already near the top of my Jerk List, Leonard. A few more snide remarks could see you firmly—. Wait! What was that light?"

"Lightning bug in front of your lens, probably."

"OK. That puts you at the top. Above Rashid."

"Oh…I'm all kinds of terrified over here," he replied.

"There it is again!"

"You're imagining things."

"And you're blind. Those are little green lights. Like laser guidance things. They only come out for a moment and then they're gone."

"Green lights you say? Could be Hunters. It's possible, but I think they're still occupied with systematically demolishing St. Guis's villa. Damn shame that. It made a great vacation spot. I don't suppose you'd like to tell me what happened?"

"What makes you think I know?"

"There's always a woman involved. I almost feel sorry for St. Guis, except the guy's a complete recluse and doesn't give me the time of day. Shit! That really is a green laser sight!"

"Is that bad?"

"If it's Hunters."

"There really is such a thing as a Vampire Hunter?"

"Dead serious folks, too. Won't even listen to a bribe. Too busy cleaning demons from the earth – or some other pious code they swear to."

"Will Dominick be all right?"

"Depends on how many there are. And if he's already taken out the original targets. Hmmm. Could be interesting to wait and see."

"Wait and see? Are you nuts? Dom is in trouble."

"What do you care? You were escaping him last I checked. Looks like you might get your chance."

What did she care? Emotion gripped her entire chest and started radiating from there until her fingernails even throbbed with it. She cared. A lot. That realization terrified and thrilled before turning everything into worry.

"Eleven. No. Looks like Twelve. Damn. St. Guis has his hands full tonight. He probably should change to guns. They're easier."

"He doesn't know how to shoot?"

"How would I know? The man rarely condescends to notice me. All I've ever seen him with are those swords. No…wait! Thirteen."

"Thirteen what?"

"Hunters."

Courtney was on her feet, dusting the sand from her palms onto her shorts and looking at sandals that weren't going to be easy to run in. She really needed to get some clothing that wasn't designed for leisure activities in a Mediterranean villa. When she had Dominick back in sight.

"Where do you think you're going?"

"We have to help him."

"Right. How do you imagine we do that?"

"I don't know. But we have to help him. Now! Get up and help me."

"I'm not immortal."

"You wearing a weapon for fun, or are you any good with it?" She couldn't see him stiffen at her snide tone, but it sure sounded like it.

"I work for the Vampire Assassin League for a reason, Lady. I'm one of the best."

"Then get off your butt and prove it!"

"And have my ass in a wringer when St. Guis finds out? No way. We stay here."

"Fine. Stay. I'm going in."

Courtney lost a sandal on her second step, looking and feeling like a complete idiot. It was going to take a half hour or more just to get to the bottom of this cliff. Heaven knew how long to get across the span of desert. Her eyes filled with moisture she blinked right back to where it came from. What a horrible time to find out you loved someone!

"Fine. You win. I'll get the bike. Don't move. *Women!*"

He had a dirt bike. It was loud and rough, but it was fast. It took twelve minutes to reach the compound gates and her heart kept pace with every passing second. Courtney was close to hyperventilating before they raced through them. The portal hadn't been opened. There was a huge hole cut through the chain-link topped with spiked barbed wire. She ignored it, as well as the four or five dark shadows that could be dead guards. She didn't waste any time on counting or verifying, but with all the blood, they didn't look like they were going to be a problem.

A low-pitched shriek pulsated through the night, seeming to come in waves toward them. Her heart recognized Dominick but nothing else about it was familiar. That's when she knew the full impact. She loved him. Massively. There was no fighting it anymore. It no longer mattered what he was. She loved him and somebody was hurting him.

"What is that?"

"*That* is a vampire in trouble. Bail!"

Courtney didn't have time to register the command before the bike went left, and Len launched right, taking her with him. Her hip took the brunt of the impact, while a spear-thing stabbed into the ground where they'd just been. She watched with gap-mouthed shock as Len had his rifle off his shoulder, pegged the spear-thrower as well as the man behind him. He'd done it so rapidly the shaft of the spear was still trembling.

"Move!"

He didn't have to say that twice. Bullets whizzed past her, making air-rifle sounds. They had silencers. Great. Courtney scrambled toward a building, hitting the side of it exactly like Len did, with the same thump.

"What's with the spears?"

"Not just spears. These are made of wood…from a cross. Very effective at killing vampires. If aimed right. Run!"

Another spear sliced through the air above her left ear. It went wide since she crouched low, learned from hours of playing VIDWAR. Instinct kicked in. Courtney ran, stumbled over a fallen body, rolled, and grabbed for his weapon before she reached her feet again. Dodged behind a Quonset hut and checked the gun. She had a 9mm. Clip intact. Fully loaded. She'd lost both sandals and the shorts were ripped, but they were small prices to pay.

Another shriek pierced the air, sending a chill all the way through her. Courtney swallowed the emotion back, blinked away any tears, steadied her hands, sucked in a deep breath, and then raced for the sound. She didn't know where Len was, and she didn't care.

She ran into another body, this time going to her knees in a jolt that had nothing elegant about it. Another guard fellow. Headless. Courtney ignored the gore and grabbed for his weapon as well. And his spare clip. She tucked it into her waistband. The hum of voices drew her to a large building shape, the door just barely cracked, letting a slice of light onto the dirt outside. Courtney heard a groaning sound from Dom and then she was at the door. She knew they were Hunters without looking. There was an unpleasant burnt smell in the air about them.

"You're killing him!"

"That's the idea."

"We need him alive! That's the lone way to find their leader."

"Alive? The bastard's too dangerous. You want to risk it? Look around. He's already taken out half the team."

"I say fry him."

"Then we have to wait for another bit of luck. I don't know about you, but I'm sick to death of following Leonard Griggins around. Three months of sick."

"It worked."

"Yeah…this time."

"I say we kill him."

Courtney's entire body tensed. She had to wipe her palms on her shorts and re-grip her guns. Right first. Left.

"Not until he talks!"

"Use the Holy water, already. It'll burn right through him. They tell me it's agonizing. He'll talk."

"Allow me."

She heard sizzling and then something suspiciously like a sob. Courtney peeked; retreated back into the shadow. That one look told her enough. There were seven of them. One was dripping water onto Dom. The rest were in various stages of amusement. *Chuckling.* They wore dun-colored uniforms of some kind, matching the surroundings. They had spear-things and guns. They had every light in the place lit. Dom was in the center of them, covered in some netting thing, while two spears projected from him. He was in a heap.

Keep your cool, Courtney. Evaluate. React.

She stepped into the warehouse; aimed both guns; waited until they all looked over at her. Most of their expressions were ludicrous.

"Evening gentlemen."

"What the fu—?"

It was the guy with the water. Courtney nailed him mid-forehead before his gun finished clearing his holster. She had her sights aimed at two others before the man fell. She almost smiled at the shock on their faces. She wasn't a VIDWAR Gray Class marksman for nothing.

"Anyone else want to try me?" she asked, flicking her eyes to the others.

The heap that was Dom shifted, and then trembled. Good. He still lived. Or whatever vampires did. *Soon, my love. Soon.*

"You want to just pack up and leave now? Or you want to play?" She continued.

"Go away, Little Girl. We got things to do."

The man on her far right said it with his move to shoot. Courtney pegged him in the chest and then the left eye. Just to show she could. She didn't wait for him to crumple before moving her sights again.

"I said release him. Now."

"You don't understand! He's a vamp—!"

She had him and the guy beside him who tried to get a shot off, both of them mid-chest, and then center forehead. She'd heard dead silence was an accolade, carrying respect; awe. She was finally receiving it. There wasn't a sound coming from anyone.

"I already know he's a vampire. Now…is someone going to take the covering off him, or do I have to make you?"

One of them shifted his eyes. A whiff of ash-tainted odor added to it. Courtney hit the ground on a knee, spun, and shot the man in the door through the groin and then his open mouth. She didn't have to duck to avoid the spear sent at her, but did it anyway, regaining her feet to face the others again. It looked like those three hadn't even moved.

"I'm really getting tired of asking. You."

She gestured with her left gun at the left man. He moved to Dom and pulled at the netting. One part of her noted it had crucifixes dangling from the under-side of it; hundreds of them, each burning and scraping as they moved. The other part of her was steel-hard and lethal. Dominick looked like a piece of raw meat. The two spears went through his chest. All the way through it. Courtney clamped her jaw to keep the cry from sounding. The guns wavered. She tightened everything: her fingers on the triggers, her forearms, back, legs. The muscles behind her eyes joined in, giving everything an odd reddish hue.

"You have one chance left, Gentlemen. You can drop your weapons and leave, and nobody else has to die."

"Who are you?" One of them asked.

"Me? Can't you tell? I'm his mate."

She should've known they wouldn't leave nicely. Courtney watched them all act as one, on a silent signal. Idiots. She'd passed that test in the Yellow Class phase. She had them all nailed and didn't need Len's bullet adding to her final shot, but it was nice to know he'd arrived finally. He moved to stand beside her as the last man dropped onto his face.

"Holy smoke, Sister. Remind me not to get between you and your mate."

Courtney didn't answer. She'd ditched the guns and was beside Dominick, finding his jaw and lifting his face, looking for his eyes. No spark of life. Just obsidian black. Nothing.

"I called for a chopper."

"What?" She wasn't really listening. Dom wasn't responding.

"We have to evacuate. Rapidly. Doesn't look like His Highness is ready…and there's that anonymous 911 call to consider."

"You made a 911 call?"

"Somebody's got to let those cult members out of the lock-up. And look there. We got dead Hunters all over the place to take the blame this time."

"What should…I do?" Courtney was sobbing. She couldn't hide it. She wasn't a merciless killer in the VIDWAR game anymore. She was a woman in love and it was a horrible feeling. And if Dominick died, she was going with him.

"We have to get those stakes out of him. It'll really hurt. You're not going to shoot me when I do it, are you?"

"No."

"Good. Hold him then. Tight."

Courtney grabbed onto Dom while Len moved behind, put a boot to Dom's back and yanked. Warm fluid spurted. Life fluid. Courtney couldn't see it through her tears. It was enough she knew what it was.

"Good! Now…the other one."

The second spear took three solid yanks. Dom's body jerked each time before it was out. Courtney was beyond seeing, no matter how she blinked, more tears got in the way. Dom coughed. Shuddered.

"Dominick?"

Courtney lifted his chin. This time there was a life there. Or whatever vampires had.

"Hi." He smiled, but it was a sickly-looking affair. He coughed again, sending more liquid onto his chin.

"Dom! I love you! What can I do? What does he need?"

"He needs blood, Sister. I'm guessing yours." Len answered.

"Take it." Courtney brushed aside her hair, offering her throat.

"I think I'll just wait outside…if you two don't mind."

She didn't watch Len go. She watched Dominick. Even pale, with open sores all over him, he was the most handsome man she'd ever seen. And he was hers. Everything on her body knew it. All she had to do was prove it.

"Take it, Dom. Now."

"I'm…going to need all of it," he replied.

"Fine. Do it."

"Once I start…I won't be able to stop."

"*Now* you decide to use contractions. What timing."

He smiled but it was a shaky affair.

"Go on, then. Take it. I mean, that's what vampires do when they turn someone isn't it?"

"You…certain?"

"You don't think I'm staying human, do you? Honestly, Dominick Miklos St. Guis. What more do you need? I love you. I want to be with you. Forever. Starting now. Right now."

He grinned, exhibiting long, sharp fangs. Then he opened his lips, dropped his fangs to her neck, and took her.

-oOo-

A Vampire Assassin League Novella
FOREVER AS ONE

JACKIE IVIE

CHAPTER ONE

They found another body.

Dane turned the page of the well-used daily paper, glanced at the grainy photo of crime tape and a couple of Key West detectives, trying to look efficient. He grimaced. This kind of attention and interest was dangerous. Especially for him.

"Three tequila sunrises. Extra grenadine. Extra fruit. Extra orange juice. Lots of crushed ice. You know, like snow cones."

"They want any alcohol?" Dane asked.

"I think they just want to watch you move, Sweetie."

He rolled his eyes. Spring break was always the same. Different faces, same gorgeous, nearly naked bodies. None of which stirred the slightest interest from this particular bartender.

He looked over at the table where three gorgeous, barely covered coeds stood, and got three kisses blown to him.

"Did you tell them I was gay?" he asked, putting the paper away.

"Nope."

"Why not?"

"Because the big stud in the cowboy hat over in the corner told me he is…and he really thinks you're cute. Wants your number. And what time you get off."

Dane flicked a glance there. It wasn't just a big cowboy in the corner watching him - it was a big-ass one. Capable of taking down a steer or two.

"Easier to handle three little city girls than one cowboy. Know what I mean? Oh. And he wants house tap."

"It's a lager. Does he know?"

"Doesn't care. As long as you pull it, it's all good."

Dane blew out the sigh and moved to the icemaker. The cowboy looked easier to deal with. Dane could start a fight, get in a few hits, and drain some blood while he was at it. Scratch that. Cowboy was definitely harder. With the looks and size of this particular guy, it wouldn't go unnoticed. Notice was just one thing Dane avoided.

He groaned, shoveled ice into the mixer and set it atop the base.

"You know…you could try growing a scruffy beard, staying away from the gym, wearing that little sailor hat with the floppy brim again…maybe cut that mane of hair or darken it. You know, try for something other than the hard-body surfer dude look. Oh! And maybe…just maybe, you could form a few lines in your skin. You know, like normal people."

"Moisturizer," he replied, and hit the ice crusher switch.

Dangerous. If Shae noticed, others might. He'd have to move to one of his other establishments a little sooner this decade. Then, just as he hit the stop button, a tremor went right through the board floor and into him, making the blender jolt. Dane cocked his head as nonchalantly as possible toward the source.

Saw her.

And instantly recognized her. Perfectly. Completely. Relentlessly.

The woman standing there resembled a pink flamingo in a bunch of penguins. Maybe they were called a clutch. Or gaggle. Or grouping. Flock. Whatever. *Doesn't frickin' matter, Dane.* She was his mate, as sure as they were both standing there. She'd arrived in his sphere! Emotion pumped through him, forcing him to stifle it, tamp the grin and tighten every muscle. Who cared that she wore a classic tailored dark blue business suit with little spectator pumps and actual hose on her legs in a tropical bar in Florida? She existed! After a millennia of time!

He didn't just recognize her. Every cell on his body flamed into a lifelike state at occupying the same chunk of real estate with her. His hand shook wildly, shifting ice right out of the blender. Dane grabbed three tall tumblers and sent the ice there, as if he'd planned it.

"Now, that's something you don't see every day," Shae remarked.

"No lie," he muttered.

"You. Being clumsy. And looking kind of…thunderstruck."

"Go get her seated. At a good table. And get her order."

"Who?"

"The woman."

"There's over fifty patrons already tonight, Dane. Thanks to the view – and I'm not talking the ocean here – most of our customers are women. You want to be just a little more specific?"

Dane finished filling the plastic glasses with ice, sent two tablespoons of grenadine, five ounces of orange juice, a half-shot of tequila, a splash of blue triple sec, not only for color but to create a nice marinade float for the three spears of pineapple, orange slice, and maraschino cherry that decorated the tops, and then placed them with precision on Shae's tray. All without measuring.

"The one by the pole. In the suit." He slanted a nod in that direction before pulling up a draught of lager in a huge frosted mug, and adding it to her tray.

"Someone is wearing a—? Oh. Got her."

"Just get her order. Here." Dane lifted the tray with the slowest, easiest, movement he could manage. It still slammed onto the bar surface in front of Shae.

"You got a thing for expensive call girls?"

"She's not a call girl."

"And you would know this…how?"

Shae shouldered the tray, ignoring his reply, or even if he'd formulated one. She was a great waitress, with tips to validate it. She had long legs, and a swinging walk that was heightened by the mid-thigh-length khaki shorts she wore. Sandals, white braided rope belt, and a neon purple and red tropical shirt with sleeves almost to the elbow finished her uniform. It matched all the waitresses tonight. As well as his other bartenders, Sam and Lyle, down flirting with girls at the other side of the bar. His employees called their shorts long and unfashionable. The shirts got the same disdain. Didn't change it. The length was the only way Dane could disguise a thigh-high tan and biceps that belonged on a body builder. That's what came of wearing tunics in his former life and pushing oars for weeks on end. Dane smirked as he watched Shae delivering drinks before speaking to the woman. His employees didn't complain after the first couple of days. The uniform actually made them look professional, in a Florida beach bar sort of way. Anybody can show skin. Few can show it effectively.

Shae had pegged the trouble with his hair, too, but there wasn't much he could do about it. Nothing changed it. It was still mid-back length, honey-blond, and thick. He'd been in perfect fashion in the 1970s. Now, he looked like he grew it out for the statement it made. That's why it was in a tail, tucked into the back of his shirt. He'd even had it cut and spiked and tipped with bleach one evening during the Y2K celebration. What happened? Upon his awakening the next night, it was back to exactly the same length and color.

Shae escorted his mate over to a table not near enough to him, waiting until she got seated before taking an order. Wow. He was one lucky surfer-dude looking guy. She was gorgeous and had great legs. That dark blue pencil skirt just emphasized it. And he'd had it wrong. She was definitely the penguin – all class and sass - in an entire bar full of colorful birds of paradise.

She was probably shy. Her attire screamed uptight New Englander, with lineage probably harkening to the Mayflower landing. Conservative. Distinguished. Classy. She looked older than his twenty-four years, too. The bun she'd forced her hair into might be emphasizing that, though. But he had nothing against older women. Should his mate be a grand-mother, he'd embrace her as perfection. He'd just change her as soon as possible to prevent further aging. Besides, he hung with these crowds because that's where his appearance best fit in, not because he was young. Dane slit his eyes and watched his mate, doing his best to give the appearance of nonchalance, and failing miserably. Despite everything, his entire frame focused on her, sending waves of hypnotic vibes toward her. He found her heartbeat, distinct and different even among so many others…the quickening pace calling to him. Searching for him. Already owning and claiming him…

Both Shae and the woman looked over at him. Dane moved with a blur to the middle of the bar, where another waitress was just giving her order. It was better to look busy.

Focus, Dane. Yeah. Focus. How the hell was he supposed to do that?

"Lemon vodka and tonic, pina colada, and a beer with lime."

"What kind of colada?" he asked.

"She doesn't care as long as 'Dane makes it'."

Linda was his oldest waitress. Steady. Thirty-three. Not prone to falling for her boss. Thank goodness. He had enough trouble. She had a sarcastic bent to her, though, as evidenced by her mimicry of a high-pitched girl voice. Dane sighed heavily, and then looked to the wooden roof joists. Sam snickered at his elbow, adding to his audience.

"So tell me Sport, how's it feel being a sex magnet?"

"I'll trade." Dane grabbed the vodka and rum bottles, poured a good shot of vodka into one glass, added the rum to another blender full of ice. They were getting a crushed ice colada, and it was going to be strawberry. Just because that's the first thing he grabbed.

"Sorry. Don't have your build. Or your looks. And don't get me started on the hair." Sam doffed his cap, showing a receding hairline and then plopped it back on.

"Well, I think you're gorgeous, Sam."

Linda blew him a kiss, and Sam grinned. Dane shook his head and hit the blender switch to drown them both out. Sex and Sunburn. Served nightly. It wasn't just the name of the establishment. It was in the air.

"Yo! Dane!"

Shae was back, leaning over the counter like she had a secret to impart. Dane's ears pricked up over the noise of the blender. He tipped his head to her and sharpened his hearing to the extent the sighs from his three coed admirers were audible.

"Appears the attraction you feel is mutual, Love."

Dane's eyes went wide. And before he could formulate a reply, Sam answered.

"Whoa. News flash. I repeat. News. Flash. Did you say *mutual?* And attraction? In the same sentence? With our Dane? I got to see this."

"Where is she? And who?" Lyle added.

"I'd rather know what," said Linda.

"No way." That was Marcy, another waitress, joining the throng.

Great. He had an audience. Damn everything. Dane killed the switch on the blender base; fought the influx of fluid hitting his nose with a needle-like sensation, setting off bells and ringing and fire bursts inside him just like the pinball machines in the corner; tightened everything against the immediate flash of real, human, physical reaction hitting all the way through him. Over just a few words. His attraction was mutual? Wow. How was he to stifle the immediate actual joy?

Focus, Dane.

What the hell? Nothing worked. Everything was going crazy inside him and nothing he tried worked to halt it. The blender handle cracked and then broke off within his fingers. Dane tossed it in the trash and poured the mixture with a hand around the container.

"Show off," Sam remarked.

"She order a drink?"

"Nope. Just…you. At her table. At your convenience."

The blender tipped, sending the last of the mixture in a rush that overran the tumbler. Dane grabbed for a towel. Blotted the mess. Put the drink on Linda's tray. Unfastened his apron.

"Tell her to stand in line," Marcy muttered.

"And try not to look too desperate."

They didn't know. Nobody did. His spirit was soaring. He was actually surprised to still be standing with his canvas shoes atop the boards.

"You finish this for me, Sam."

Dane tossed the apron on a stool, and moved, making the end of the bar in a blur that had their mouths gaping. Great. Again. He was failing at just about everything.

"Uh...before you rush over there, I've got a quantifier to add."

Dane stopped, hovering right at the end of the bar where the pressure of his hand was putting cracks in the surface. The entire troupe made the journey along the outside of the bar, adding counter customers to their numbers. Damn it. He was gaining the one thing he most detested, and the one time he really didn't want it. Total attention. Dane gritted his teeth, felt the prick of a canine as his body already sought what only his mate could give. Succor. Bliss. And then he had to fight that, too. With an audience.

"I still want to know who. Somebody start pointing."

"Business suit. Boston bred. Can't miss her."

"Dane's got the hots for a high class call girl? What the hell?"

"She's not a call girl," he replied. It came through clenched teeth, so he wasn't surprised to see a few raised brows.

"Yeah. Who knew? All this time we thought—"

"What was the quantifier?" he asked, more to stop their speculating than because he wanted to know.

"Well…she didn't actually ask for you. Not by name, anyway."

"Who needs his name? The Viking stud at the bar usually works," Marcy offered.

"Not even that. She wants to talk to the owner of this place. And that's you. Sorry. I didn't know it mattered so much."

Ah…deflation. Thy name is woman.

Dane fought such supreme disappointment he was probably in full snarl. It was better to watch the floor, where little bits of sand glimmered with light from the fake flickering torches. His failure was going to be complete if the ledge in his hand broke off. He'd failed at hiding his superior strength. He was failing at hiding his reaction to a let-down. He was failing at hiding. Period.

"So? You going over there? Or you want me to fill in for you again?"

Sam had obviously finished filling the drink order. Dane watched his apron get pitched across the bar, landing atop his hand, right where he needed it. If he relaxed his grip slowly, the creak of wood might not give away the enormous chunk he'd probably ripped loose. If he concentrated, he could still hear his mate's heart-rate, elevated now. It might have something to do with the spectacle he was making. He sent a tongue over his teeth, checked for elongation, and then lifted his head.

"I'll handle it. Thanks. As for the rest of you? Get back to work."

It was a futile order. It didn't work like in the movies. Nobody did anything other than stand aside, opening an aisle right to her table. Or perhaps it was better described as a gauntlet, since even customers pitched in, closing in both sides. There was nothing for it. For someone avoiding attention, it was ludicrous. Dane stepped into the void, heard the chunk of wood fall, and then put his entire attention on her.

His mate.

Her heart rate got even faster, and skipped more than once as he approached, all of which she hid beneath a well-polished exterior. She was good. Really good. Only the slightest tint of blush hitting her cheeks showed her agitation. He just didn't know if it was his approach, or the crowd he'd managed to gather about them.

He slid the opposite chair out, flipped it backwards, and slouched into it, laced his hands through the lattice work at the back, working at his best impression of a lazy rich man. He added to it by tipping his chin down, and waited, watching her through his eyelashes.

Wow! He wasn't just lucky. He'd hit the mother lode. She was a pure beauty, without a touch of cosmetic enhancement. Pale, unblemished skin like hers would've made her a favorite at any medieval court. Her hair looked to be a rich brown, the match to her eyelashes. She brought her glance to him and completely stole what was left of his senses. It wasn't hurricane season, there wasn't a cloud in sight, but none of that mattered in the slightest. A roar of ocean wave lifted by a killer force of wind went right through his ears, cancelling out everything but the uptick of her heart-rate as they locked gazes.

Dane had vivid blue eyes. It came with his heritage. He'd heard more than enough about them over the centuries, but hers! Hers were almost indescribable...a dark gray-blue, the near match to her suit. Unfathomable. Showing depths to be plumbed. Fathoms of mystery to delve. He was hooked. Reeled in. Netted.

"Hi."

She may have said it. He might even have heard it. Her lips moved, catching his glance to their honeyed appearance. Everything that was male on him went rigid. Instantly and immediately. Without one bit of instruction or intent. He was grateful for the position that hunched him forward, hiding a reaction from so far in his past he'd forgotten how it felt. Lips like hers demanded his kiss. Tormented. Teased. Invited. They were ripe. Lush. Full. Feminine. Immeasurably sweet.

She lifted a hand to move a strand of hair from atop her lash, the movement caught a flash, and Dane's entire being ratcheted into something so immense, there wasn't any way to fight it. He recognized it, too. Supreme male dominated rage.

She wore a wedding ring.

CHAPTER TWO

Vangie had taken this job because it sounded interesting. Easy. A walk in the park. Fly down to Florida; during spring break no less. Find the bar called Sex and Sunburn. Find the owner. He's named Morgan. Likes the party crowd. Usually works behind the counter of his own bar. Meet him. Schmooze him about the possibility of selling. Get a price range. Communicate. Bargain. Seal the deal with a handshake. Her employers had sweetened the offer with a bonus of 1% for every dollar under twenty million she managed to negotiate. It was right up her alley. She even had a degree in business, and listed her specialty as corporate negotiation.

She was also lying to herself. Still. Again.

She took this third job from this same shady company because it was very expensive to live after Rod's death wiped her out and nobody else offered, no matter how many times she reworded her resume, or how many places she submitted it to. She was already working two minimum wage jobs; both part-time, one handling night-shift at the local convenience store, because nobody offered full time work with benefits anymore.

This time her employers had even thrown in travel expenses, to Key West of all places, Florida per diem rates which were exorbitant, and they gave her a big enough advance she splurged on Italian spectator pumps to wear with her one good suit. Easy money. Perfect for her qualifications. If she turned a blind eye to things like cash transactions and amounts that never went above nine thousand, nine-hundred and ninety-nine dollars. For a law-abiding, uptight American, it didn't seem possible she worked to help launder money. And if she didn't watch it, her conscience would be helping her call the FBI, or something. But...not just yet. She'd be homeless if she didn't do this. It was just better to ignore the implications, follow instructions, and collect her pay.

Nobody had factored in a pissed-off, pretty-boy, ex-jock, though. And she hadn't even told him she wanted to buy his place yet.

When she'd first asked for the owner and watched the waitress go over to the most gorgeous man in existence, she'd actually got cold hands. And cold feet. And then everywhere else on her body had experienced the same sensation of ice cold chill. And excitement. Good heavens! There wasn't a guy like this in existence. Even seen at a distance, he was so perfect he looked photo-shopped. Every bit of opening conversation she'd practiced disappeared. It was difficult to breathe. The words probably didn't matter anyway. Her tongue wasn't going to work properly. Blinking hadn't muted the effect of looking at him, either. The guy was a walking piece of art with sex appeal tossed in. No wonder the place was crawling with women.

A moment ago, he'd acted ready to leap across the table and create some hot and heavy action with her – even with the crowd of people about them. And now? Now he looked like he'd just as soon rip her head off. And enjoy it.

"Uh…"

She'd been right. Her tongue didn't work. Neither did her voice. Her throat wouldn't even move on the dry swallow she sent there. He didn't need to put a finger up to stop her. That was just overkill.

"Don't say anything. Not yet. Please?"

Vangie added to her complete self-disgust by nodding. Some corporate CEO she was going to make. Someone set a tall glass in front of her, so wet with frost it darkened the napkin. She dragged her eyes from the guy across the table and managed a breath as a waitress winked at her.

"Tonic water and lemon. On the house. Sam figured you'd need it."

She did. Vangie lifted it and drank until the cold hit her brain, stopping her. When she put the glass back in place, nothing else seemed to have moved. She could feel the flush happening and didn't have anything to draw on to stop it. An introvert by nature, she'd had to work at getting to the front of her class. Speaking in public. Putting herself on display. She'd didn't want to be the center of attention. She'd always suspected it would be embarrassing. Now, she knew it was.

"Oh, everybody get back to partying! Jake, call CJ from the back. Looks like we just lost a barkeep, and I'm still needing some drinks! You? Move. You don't want me to start the boys early, do you?"

"You got this, Morgan?" That was a deeper, male voice.

The absolute god across the table grunted what might be assent. He didn't take his eyes off hers. Vangie returned the favor as if glued in place. The crowd might be moving, might even be dissolving. She couldn't say.

"All right! You were warned. Get me the boys! You're on early tonight. And make it loud!"

Laughter followed the statement. It was followed by voices, and microphone buzz, and then drumbeats invaded the entire area, reaching out from beneath the roof onto the beach beyond, pumping a rhythm that dragged her pulse with it. The beat was accompanied by a thread of melody from a reed instrument she couldn't place. Not without moving her eyes to check. Oboe, maybe? Sax? She didn't believe in magic or spirits, or mysticism, but there was something very stirring and hypnotic about the spell being woven around her. She sensed movement as shadows flitted across the span of table between them. His customers were probably dancing. Vangie didn't check that, either. The experience of gazing into his blue eyes wasn't just something magnetic, it was downright mesmeric. Tantalizing. Alluring. Enthralling. And vaguely threatening. She knew now what a rodent must feel when facing a hooded cobra.

"You ready?" he asked.

Wow. For the images that small statement caused! Beneath this suit, she wore plain white cotton briefs, white bra, nothing fancy about her slip, and yet views of red lace and naked tanned skin assailed her, coming in a rapid-fire mélange as if frames from old reel-to-reel movies were getting interspersed with reality. Vangie blinked several times, licked her lips and pulled in a breath that shuddered.

"For what?" she finally replied.

He grinned, stole her voice and her breath, and then her next heartbeat.

"Name's Dane. Dane Morgan."

Dane. *Figures.* It couldn't be something reasonable like John, or Albert. Or Henry. Oh, no. It was a name conjuring Vikings and plunder and pillaging and ravishment – as if he needed the advertisement. He put his hand out as if she'd actually touch it. And then his grin relaxed, adding stranger vibes to the mix. Vangie looked at his outstretched hand and then back at him.

"You going to tell me your name?" He dropped his hand.

She shook her head.

"Why not?"

Vangie gulped again. She should have taken another sip of her drink since her throat was so dry it scratched. She'd been naive, too. Instead of visualizing a nondescript rodent, she should have fancied herself a mongoose. Weren't they a cobra's natural enemy?

He looked away, the release granting her time to breathe, blink, and then take a gulp from her drink. In that order. *This is ridiculous, Vangie.* The guy wanted her name, not her body. Or her soul. Nothing scary about that. She'd practiced this a thousand times. Every business transaction started with the basics: Greetings. Name exchange. Handshake. She'd even been taught the correct way to shake hands. Use just a slight touch of pressure with her thumb and she wouldn't come off as a pushover or wimp. Using that method controlled "hand-crusher" types, too. They wouldn't pump her arm if she had the recurrent branch of their median nerve beneath her finger.

Besides…the worst thing that could happen is he'd tell her no. Right?

Vangie squared her shoulders, lifted her chin, and stifled her own reaction to this guy. It was ridiculous. She wasn't the type to attract gorgeous young guys, especially rich gorgeous, young guys, who looked like they spent every available moment in the company of women and more women. Surf and sand. Fun and sun. Parties and more parties. That lifestyle looked to suit him perfectly…looked really good on him, too. The tawny stripes in his hair were probably sun lightened. Or he spent a lot of time in a beautician's chair for the effect.

He didn't seem to notice her perusal. He wasn't moving. It didn't even look like he breathed, but it would be hard to note that beneath the loud colors of his shirt. It wasn't hard to define really nice pecs, wide shoulders, or the bulge of biceps in his sleeves, though. And his forearms weren't lacking in muscle, either.

She was caught as he brought his attention right back to her. There wasn't much she could do about it. It was in the warmth stealing up her breast and into her lower cheeks, but she kept her eyes on his. It felt…safer. And that was just ridiculous. She couldn't knock the sensation, though. She felt like the room spun in a wide, slow circle, trapping her in the center with a predator just hovering. Waiting. Watching. Her heart even decided to act up, dropping to somewhere within her belly, so it could pump beats from there to match the drums.

"You want to take this to my office?"

"Evangeline Harper."

He could raise just one brow at a time. His right one. And that little quirk, combined with a killer grin, was really going over the top. The room spun faster, the heart swoop happened again, only this time it took her pulse with it, starting a distinctive ringing tone in both ears with the rapidity of it. There wasn't much sense to any of this.

"Ev*an*geline."

The way he said it, with the emphasis on VAN sounded like a full skin caress. Her eyes went wide at the instant impression of fingers sliding along her knee…gliding up her thigh. They couldn't have put something in her drink…could they?

"Come on. We'll take this to my office."

"Your office?"

"Yeah. My office. Private. Quiet. Unless you like all the attention we seem to engender?"

The chair disappeared somewhere as he got to his feet, offering his hand to her again. Vangie studiously ignored it and slid her chair back. The sight of him stole her wits. She really wasn't willing to move toward touching. Not just yet. She didn't give a flying hang about polite behavior, or business etiquette, or corporate strategy, either. It was self-preservation.

Maybe she shouldn't go anywhere private and quiet with Dane Morgan. Crowds were safer. She'd read the paper, watched the news. Bodies were washing ashore lately, with shark marks that didn't disguise the bullet holes.

What was she thinking? There wasn't really an option. If they stayed here, she'd have to yell her proposal at him, and that's if she could make out his expression, since they'd started to dim the lights. She'd come down here to be exactly where she was, talking to the bar's owner and working out a deal. In fact, she was more successful than she'd dreamed. His office was a good option. Clearly. Vangie shouldered her purse strap and stood.

Dane Morgan was over six feet tall. *That figures, too*. He hadn't looked that big before. He wasn't hugely muscled like a body builder, but he wasn't far behind them. She probably reached to his shoulder. Even wearing these three inch heels. Vangie took a breath and moved her gaze upward, willing the strange sensation from existence before she reached his eyes. It didn't work. She might as well be floating, along with the spinning sensation that restarted the moment she locked gazes again. She'd never felt so out-of-sorts. Disconnected. Uninhibited.

"Take my hand. Please?"

That right eyebrow lifted again, and he tipped his head lower to speak just to her.

"I—"

"I don't bite. Not on a first meeting, anyway. Promise."

Mongoose, Vangie. Make like a mongoose. What a stupid idea. Mongoose moved lightning fast. That's how they avoided being caught by a cobra's stare. Or she hadn't paid enough attention to those nature films back in grammar school. Nothing about her felt like moving at all, let alone quickly.

"Did they put something in my drink?"

His lips twitched, but at least he didn't smile. "Why?"

"Because I feel…." Her words dragged into nonexistence. There wasn't a description to this. She'd never taken a mood enhancement drug. She'd been around those who did, though, back when she tried to fit in and failed miserably. It had been a learning experience. She never wanted to be out of control of her own body. Like now. *Just great Vangie. Great.* She not only appeared to be easily influenced, she looked mindless as well.

"Take my hand."

"I'll follow."

That got her another grin. "In this crowd? I'll lose you. Come along. I promise you'll be safe."

"Right." He might lose her, but he'd be impossible to mistake.

"You don't believe me?"

"Should I?" Good. Her mind still worked, and it controlled her words. She almost let the self-satisfaction show before catching it.

"Did you wish to speak with me, or not?"

Trust a man to find the loophole. He was right. She was being paid to be right where she was. Privacy would be perfect, quiet even better. And he was offering both. She took his hand, got a jolt all the way through to the tips of her pinched toes in her shoes and back, and it was followed by such a sensation of heat, she almost snatched her hand back. He may have known, too, for the next moment found her entire form against what she'd suspected was a rock hard physique. Now, she knew it was.

They'd definitely put something in her drink. Otherwise, how could they be in a near-embrace and surrounded by writhing bodies in a crowded darkened club one moment, and the next out on shadowy open beach spliced by moonlight through palm fronds? And why wasn't she finding it the slightest bit difficult to walk in wet sand with these heels?

Vangie glanced down.

She wasn't touching the sand. He had her in his arms, and was moving so fast, they might as well be flying. She slammed her eyes shut and swallowed over and over. She was going to be airsick. Nobody had thought of that. The thud of steps on wood startled her, and worked at settling her belly. Good. He'd reached wood. Solidness. And he wasn't flying. She peeked.

They were at the end of a dock. He owned a sleek, black boat, very hard to see at night. She thought they were called cigar boats. At least, that's what she remembered from the movies. She probably should've spent more time in pursuit of a social life, and less time with television and her imagination, because whatever they'd given her was really warping reality, and she had a lot of imagination to draw from. Either that or he really did own a boat so fast, it flew, too. Without lights. Without much noise. Without even making a drop of sea spray. She didn't have time for seasickness before a large black shape loomed out of the night sky all about them, sending a wave to rock the boat as they neared.

"Where the hell are we?" Forget etiquette and protocol. She was angry, and it showed in her words and her voice.

"My office."

"Bologna."

"Eric! Hit the running lights! Starboard!"

"Got it!"

Dane leaned back in order to send the commands up at more black shapes atop a railing. She couldn't see his movement, but the way he had her plastered to him, she didn't need to see it. Or anything else. She hadn't imagined all that muscle and hard ripped body, either. She got a full onslaught of it all along her.

She heard the sound of chains scraping, a hiss of noise, some shouts, and then one side of the most enormous yacht she'd ever seen up close came into view, lit by blue-enhanced lights. The entire side facing them was black. Sleek, shiny black. And way at the top were large painted white letters along with his call numbers. It wasn't hard to read them, even from this angle.

My Office.

"You see?"

Jerk. He should just keep his mouth shut. Dane Morgan wasn't just a pretty-boy, rich, surfer dude. He was a complete and total jerk, too. Vangie cleared her throat to give her best "we can't come to an agreement" spiel. She was usually very good at it.

"Look...Mister Morgan. We got off on the wrong foot. I've changed my mind. I want to go back to shore. I'll save my words for another day. When you're not so busy. So...say you just turn this little boat of yours around and take me back. Okay? I'll be back tomorrow and we can—just what do you think you're doing?"

Leaping upward without one bit of assist, and then walking into an enormous salon place with her was what he did. He deposited her onto an overstuffed leather sofa, and then took a seat right beside her. Then he turned toward her as if she was the most important thing in the world. And if she didn't do something to stop this, she'd probably be assailed with the hypnotic sensation again. Vangie sucked in a breath, held it, and then slammed her eyes shut. She wasn't making eye contact with him. No way. The man was pure drug to her, and she was acting like a full-fledged addict.

He put a finger beneath her chin and lifted it, sparking something right through her that had nothing to do with prior experience. Nothing. Vangie started silently counting. She got to three before he picked up her right hand within his, sending flurries of shivers with the contact. She was never trusting another man. Ever. Never. Ever. And if she got out of this, she was never ever taking another job without checking every single bit of their credentials, either. *And* she was calling the feds.

" *Frja*? I cannot believe it. You exist. And you're here. With me."

She cracked open an eye. He had his one eyebrow cocked up again and the strangest expression on his face. Vangie opened the other eye to view what looked like tenderness and something else. Something akin to awe. Reverence. Wonder. The moist sheen atop his eyes seemed to reflect it, as well. And damn everything, she got to turn into his willing prey again, immediately drawn to the bottomless blue of his eyes.

"Finally. I simply cannot believe it. I can't."

"I…shouldn't be here." It was her mouth speaking, but she couldn't truly feel her lips and throat making the sounds.

"You fear me?"

Fear? What a word for so vast an experience. He upset the very elements, altered them, and then reassembled them back in such a haphazard fashion, she didn't know what to think or believe.

"I don't know. I don't think so. Should I?"

"You're perfectly safe with me. You will always be safe."

"After a trick like you just pulled, how am I supposed to believe that?"

"What trick?"

He actually had the gall to look confused. Vangie blinked around the blurred aura that seemed to surround them, but couldn't move her eyes from his. Damn everything! She'd known not to lock gazes with him!

"This…is not your office," she whispered.

"It is."

"It's a yacht."

"What does that matter? It's quiet and private, just as I offered."

"Exactly. Perfect for all kinds of things…like—"

Red lace and entwined limbs. Naked, tanned skin…. Candlelight. Satin sheets.

The same images assailed her again in disjointed snippets that had perfect clarity to them. It was worse than before, and so much better. Her head tipped back slightly while her eyelids drooped. Her lips parted to pant for breath. His fingers about her hand tightened. Everything about him looked to have the same affliction – all taut and muscled and ready to spring – and the shirt wasn't hiding one bit of it.

"This is not a good idea." He looked down at the hand he held. His voice was rough as he stated the obvious.

"No. Yes."

"I was a fool to bring you here. And yet…what else was I to do?"

"Mister Morgan?"

"Dane."

She ignored his name, and the little smile he gave. It only worked because he was still speaking to her fingers. "We should…go back."

"You are safer with me than with any other creature on the planet. I vow it." He polished off that statement by lifting her hand and placing a kiss right atop the ridges of her knuckles.

Oh my…heavens! No wonder they'd loved that gesture in the middle ages! The spark that shot from that spot went straight to her center, starting a tremor that was noticeable. Her hand shook within his, and her entire frame wasn't far behind. She held her breath. He lifted his eyes back to hers.

"I must leave you now, *Frja*. I cannot stay near you, and not—! I cannot control—! You do not understand…and I cannot explain. Forgive me."

He dropped her hand and was gone, leaving total chill in his wake. In a blink of time. Without making a hint of sound. Not a footstep. Not a door closure. Nothing.

CHAPTER THREE

This wasn't a yacht. It was more a ship. She'd once thought being on a ghost ship would be cool. She'd been a lot younger then. A little less world-weary. Rod had been the neighbor's kid, not her deceased husband. They'd both shared an interest in the strange and scary. She supposed it started when he'd found a book about the Flying Dutchman and crew that disappeared in 1795. It had been spotted lots of times since, but never verified. Sounded really cool.

Ghost ships weren't as fun once she got older and saw some of the horror movies. Then they were just plain spooky. Spooky. With a capital S.

That description was more than apt. This one probably even echoed.

Vangie peeked around a corner and got a dose of more corridor, acreage of charcoal-hued carpeting, dark wood paneling, and the same sparkling chrome fixtures. Didn't matter if she found a staircase and went up or down, either. Everything started looking alike. He had at least three decks. She hadn't gone down the last set of steps because she was afraid of getting lost. They'd looked different. They weren't carpeted and the walls below looked like white paint covered them. She probably should have dared it.

"See, this is the problem with rich people."

She said it aloud. It helped curb the sensation that was raising hairs at the back of her neck. Vangie gestured to the hall as she lectured.

"They can't take it with them, so they design monstrosities like this to spend their money on. Expensive cars, huge mansions, elaborate estates, yachts the size of cruise ships. And then they have to buy privacy fences. Security forces. Electronic surveillance stuff…"

If she ever had a fortune at her command – which wasn't likely given her success rate tonight – she'd find a way to make the money work for her. Better people's lives. Work on the environment. Make a difference. Something other than waste it on something that sooner or later was going to end up a chunk of rusting iron on the ocean floor, doing more damage than good.

"I mean…just look at this. The guy has a lot of space. And for what? Parties? Privacy? Status? What a waste."

Her voice drifted off. She'd been right. It echoed, and did nothing to temper the shivers.

She ran a finger along the slick chrome rail next. Not a speck of dust, either. He kept it perfectly maintained. Figures. He probably paid an army of servants to keep it in this condition. They must sleep during the night, unlike their employer. That didn't automatically mean if she'd gone down that odd staircase, she wouldn't find a living being or two.

Maybe.

Vangie peeked around the next corner, and then looked back the way she'd come. The view was exactly the same. Great. She was lost. Some of the doors had markings on them, but they weren't numeric, so she hadn't paid attention. She pulled her cell phone from her purse and turned it on.

Roaming.

Fine. Roam away. Just get her a bar or two and she'd be happy. Heck, at this point, she'd settle for access to the GPS. Heck, she might need a GPS just to find the salon he'd left her in. This was ridiculous. And her phone was taking forever.

No Service.

"You must be Ms. Harper."

Vangie squealed, dropped her purse and phone, and spun. The giant of a man standing behind her wasn't remotely handsome. But he was real. And human. And he found her antics very funny if the grin on his face was an indication.

"Sorry. I didn't mean to startle you."

"Who...are you?"

"Sven Haardrasson."

"Scandinavian?"

"Swede. How did you know?" he asked.

"Lucky guess." Vangie bent in the most ladylike fashion she could manage wearing a tight blue dress suit to retrieve her phone, a stray tube of lip gloss, and her little purse. She addressed her next remarks to the carpet at his feet. He had big feet, too. "Sven. Erick. Dane. Is everybody here from the North?"

"Mostly. We make good seamen."

"Pillaging, plundering, rampaging...kidnapping. The Viking era is over, you know."

"You ready yet?"

"For what?" No images came to her this time. Obviously it was just Dane who could control that part of her mind. That wasn't comforting, but at least it could be managed.

"I've been sent to find you."

Vangie waited to get back upright, and then stood with her back against the corner, reaching for her fullest height. It was easier to talk to him that way, even if she did look to be straining for a few extra centimeters. "Oh. My transport must be ready."

"Transport?"

"Back to shore. Didn't Mister Morgan tell you?"

"Dane?"

"Is there anyone else named Morgan aboard?"

"No."

"Then yes. I'm talking about that Mister Morgan."

There were stupid conversations, and then there were 'going nowhere' stupid conversations. This was the latter. Vangie waited while he assimilated her statement. Okay. The guy was big. Muscled. Not very handsome, and not very bright. But he knew his way about the ship. And he could probably be manipulated. Vangie glanced up at him and smiled slightly.

"He didn't tell you to ready a transport for me?"

"Follow me."

He didn't wait to see if she'd obey, he simply turned down the corridor she'd been in and expected she'd follow. And she did.

He led her along what felt like another quarter mile of hallway, up two staircases that didn't resemble anything she'd traversed earlier – they were wider and even more elegant – and then waited for her to catch up. Damn heels.

"Can I ask you something?"

He nodded.

"What on earth are the markings on all the doors?"

"Runic symbols."

"Runic? As in *Viking* Runic? And you can actually read them?"

He sighed, moving a lot of chest. "See that plate on the doorframe beside the handle?"

She did. It read 212. In normal numeric form.

"That shows we're on the second deck. Twelve doors from the stern. Come along now. Dane doesn't like to be kept waiting."

"So?"

Getting kidnapped, held hostage aboard a ghost ship, and then scared wasn't doing her sense of protocol and etiquette any good. It did wonders for her impatience and frustration, though.

"So, hurry."

"Or what?"

"Or, he'll see me punished."

"Right. Like I...believe that." The words were split with the way she stopped for breath between them, since she had to jog the steps to reach where he stood.

"Why wouldn't you?"

"Because lazy...rich...playboys aren't...the type to administer punishments. You'd have to...practice discipline first." And if she wasn't panting, it would have made more sense.

"Not him. The Captain. And I like shore leave."

Likely story. But what did she know about it? A ship this size probably needed a crew to man it. They might even have a captain that disciplined offenses. Shore leave might be a rare event, because just maybe they stayed out to sea most of the time.

"Then why are you here now? Seems to me, you'd be on shore partying like the rest of the world. Oh no. No. Please, don't say it. He wouldn't."

At the thought, the slightest lurch happened, as if engines were starting up, or an anchor had been pulled, or they'd started moving. And if Dane thought he could put out to sea with her, he obviously didn't know a thing about women, and less about New Englanders. And Sven here wasn't going to be any help.

"That's it. I'm done with nonsense. Just where is Mister Morgan hiding?"

They reached two enormous wooden doors with matching chrome handles on them. Dead center. She was the seasick type. She didn't take a honeymoon cruise for that reason. Mongoose, my ass. He was about to meet the mother of angry: a pissed-off New Englander. There was a reason the Revolutionary War started there.

Sven knocked loudly on one side of the door. Vangie turned the handle on the other one, pushed it open, and stomped in. Or tried to stomp. The carpeting in here was even thicker than that in the halls. Her heels sank into luxury that ruined any aggressive entrance. And the man getting to his feet over by a really ornate fireplace didn't look like anyone to argue with.

He'd swapped the shorts for long dark thigh-hugging denims and the loud tropical shirt for a blue t-shirt that molded to a torso Michelangelo couldn't improve while showing off more toned arms than before. And his hair! Even with it pulled back, his honey-shaded hair was so dark and shiny it looked wet.

Her heart decided to torment her with another low swoop to the pit of her belly. She'd forgotten his effect on her.

And his handsomeness.

Damn it. Damn it. Damn it.

"Evangeline. You're back."

"Turn...this ship around." The first word came out exactly as she meant it. The last part of her sentence limped out like wet noodles.

"Hard to do," he answered. "Sven?"

"We aren't moving. You want to give the signal?"

"Not yet."

"You got this, Boss?"

Vangie swiveled to face the giant holding the door open. "He's not going to need your assistance, Sven. Not at the moment. But don't go hiding, okay? You hear him screaming, you come running. Got it?"

"Dane?"

"You heard the lady."

Sven saluted her before shutting the door. She distinctly heard the sound of a lock clicking into place. She was getting locked in, too? And they weren't moving? The strangest vibration was coming through the soles of her feet, defying that. They were moving, or she was losing her mind.

"Why did he lock it?"

She sent the words at the closed and locked doors. It was easier to speak if she didn't look at Dane while she did so.

"It's not locked."

"Right."

"You don't believe me?"

"Heck no. I don't trust you, either."

"You don't trust me?"

Vangie turned around slowly. It wasn't an elegant move. Her shoes didn't slide against the carpet so she had to pivot by lifting them in little steps. It put him back in her direct line of sight, too, and that just rattled words off her tongue.

"You tricked me onto your yacht, you disappeared and from the looks of things took a swim in the ocean, and now you're keeping me against my will. What part of that is trustworthy, Mister Morgan?"

"It wasn't a trick. And it's Dane."

"Right."

"You're also not being held against your will. You're free to leave…just as soon as we conclude our business."

"Oh. Really."

"We should be done by dawn."

"Dawn," she repeated.

"In about five hours the sun will rise, and it will be a new day. If you wish, you can leave then. You have my word."

"Five hours?"

"A pittance."

He waved a hand to demonstrate the loss of a good portion of her sleep time. Vangie's lips tightened. He might be jaw-dropping handsome, but the longer she was around him, the easier it was to form words and make sense.

"You'll have a hard time ordering that if you take another ocean swim, won't you?" She didn't know why she still grumbled. He was being fairly amenable. And so far, he hadn't done anything threatening. Or anything approaching ravishment.

"I wasn't in the ocean. The water isn't cold enough."

Her mouth opened and nothing came out. She had to shut it or remain affixed in that position. What he implied wasn't possible. It just *wasn't*.

"I can't promise I won't leave you again, either. I may need to. Do you play chess?"

"Chess?"

He moved sideways, revealing a heavy wooden table with what might be a chess board and pieces atop it. Only it looked massive enough to be used as a prop in an Olympian movie. The pieces looked over six inches high each, and carved into some sort of Arabian looking figures. The bases might be black and white but the rest were painted with all sorts of colors, while what was probably real gold trim lined every bit of clothing on the figurines.

She should have paid attention in her archeology classes. They looked like something from…the Ottoman Empire or Arabian Nights or something. Her feet moved without her instruction and within moments she was at the table, with Dane on her right side. Up close, his chess pieces were even more impressive.

"Where did you get this?" She was awe-struck. Her voice carried every bit of it.

"Constantinople."

She shook her head. "Don't you mean Istanbul?"

"Oh. Yes. My mistake. Istanbul. You wish white or black?"

He bent forward, extending his arms across the chess board as if to swivel it. That was too much man and too nicely arrayed. *Wow.* She'd never seen such a physique, and he wielded it so easily, without thought to any consequence! Vangie's eyes widened and she gasped. This was ridiculous behavior. If he chanced a glance at her, there wouldn't be much way to hide it. She was staid, proper. Even Rod called her frigid. Nothing about her life triggered massive heat and sensual awareness. Until now.

"Leave…it." Her voice was breathless. Panted.

"Black, then?"

Vangie slid around the table, gaining space from his proximity. She needed it before looking up at him. She'd been wrong. The sensations he evoked in her weren't just ridiculous and impossible. They were insane. He had to possess the deepest, bluest eyes on record. Not just vivid blue…but deep. Dark. Mysterious. Little dots hampered her view and they were accompanied by a sway into the table. Vangie gripped the edge with both hands to catch what felt like a swoon.

"You're making this very difficult for me, *Frja.*"

She thought he said it, but his lips didn't do more than mold into a perfect kiss shape. He couldn't possibly mean he was having the same difficulty? Could he?

"I have given my word."

"About…what?" Her voice was a sigh of sound.

His face showed pain before he lowered his head. Every muscle on him tightened until he resembled one of the chess pieces. And then he straightened, opened his eyes, and looked at her with a completely blank expression.

"If you take black, I get the opening move."

"Opening move?" Why didn't that make sense?

"Chess." He dropped his eyes to the board between them.

"Oh. Right. You want to play chess."

"Yes."

"I don't do well with chess. Even if I'm wide awake. And right now, it's sleep-thirty. I mean, you already called it. It's past two. In the morning."

"I'm a night person."

"Figures. Well. If you want to play chess, I'm willing, but I'm not going to give you a very good match."

"Really? Why?"

She sighed. Men. Seriously.

"Aren't you listening? Chess requires concentration. Oh! And add in that sometimes an opponent takes so long I get bored. That makes my moves sloppy and ill-conceived. It's not that I can't play. I just lack the proper patience or something. Chess requires too much mental acuity. It can be worse than a full body workout."

"Exactly why I chose it."

That one eyebrow quirked up and sent her pulse into overdrive again, and her breathing into nonexistence. Or, maybe it was the lightning quick images that flitted through her mind again, even more visual and graphic than before. Red lace.

Satiny sheets. Candlelight. Naked, muscled skin…entwined legs. Her legs. Wrapped about him.

"Please. Sit."

His voice interrupted what was rapidly turning into an erotic fantasy for one. Her legs wobbled and she fell, and then did her best to act like she'd meant to sit that hastily. The wingback chair was upholstered in a thick damask fabric and stuffed so full, she bounced. She placed her purse on her lap and tucked her skirt around her thighs with precision while she waited for his next words. It was better than looking across the table.

"Are you right-handed?"

"What?"

She looked up and across the chess board at him. She'd been right. The pieces were about six inches tall. They were spectacularly carved, probably inlaid with real jewels, but they weren't enough to keep her from looking right at him. And getting sucked right back into the deepest, most hypnotic eyes she'd ever seen.

"I asked if you're right handed."

"I heard you. I just don't know why it matters."

"Trust me. It matters."

"Yes. I'm right handed."

He seemed to relax at that. Or she was losing her mind.

"Good."

"You're a pretty odd guy, Mister Morgan."

"Dane."

"But I suppose rich people have their eccentricities, don't they?"

"You believe in fate, Evangeline?"

"Vangie," she replied. "And no. I don't."

"Why not?"

"I believe in apple pie, and patriotism, and doing the best you can with your time on this planet. I believe in justice. And righteousness. And just plain honor and integrity. And paying your taxes. You probably don't pay taxes, do you?"

"I'm sure I do."

"See? You don't even know."

"I didn't say that. I said I'm sure I do because I've got estate executors for that."

"You've probably got loopholes to get out of it."

"You think its sheer coincidence that we met?"

Vangie licked her lips. "Wow. Talk about a one-track mind. You want to talk fate? And coincidence? Fine. But meeting you had nothing sheer about it. We're talking total coincidence here…except you need to toss in stupidity, too. We met because I took a job that I'm failing. They already paid me the advance. And here I was just talking about integrity."

"What job?"

"I need to buy your property."

"Which one?"

Vangie's expression fell. She felt it. "Which one?" she repeated.

"I have a lot of properties."

"Let me guess. You don't even know how many, do you?"

"I have estate executors for that, too."

"Figures."

"So…why don't you tell me which one you wish to purchase, and I'll consider it. And in the meantime, we'll play chess."

CHAPTER FOUR

He'd played chess for centuries; and more than once, for property. He wasn't sure how adept she'd be at the game. So Dane picked up a pawn and reflected which move would buy him the most time. Time…the one thing he'd always had so much of was now the most precious commodity in the world. He had five hours. To spend moving pieces around a chessboard, in a vain attempt to keep his thoughts from the cabin down the corridor. The one fashioned when he'd had this ship built. The suite of rooms designed just for her. It was matched in all his properties. She had rooms containing a large four-poster bed, satin sheets, gold candelabra…drawers full of red lace garments…

His hand tightened on the chess piece before he put it down. One space forward. E2 to e3. The move was against every other instinct of his heritage, and the centuries of existence since, but he automatically knew domination and annihilation weren't going to get him what he wanted.

Nothing would.

So, for a poor attempt at second best, he'd try spending what time he could with her, enjoy the absolute thrill of watching and speaking and communing silently with her, but not a moment of it touching her. And never admit to why. She didn't ask of his concern over her dexterity and which hand she favored. He wouldn't have explained. He didn't dare see the ring on her left hand again. He'd slam the chess board into oblivion. So, he studied the chess set and absorbed her presence with the best of intentions. His actions were probably labeled chivalry.

He should have known it felt as dead as the era that spawned it.

She moved her pawn d7 to d5, two spaces from his. Dane narrowed his eyes in a vain attempt to look at the board and not her. He pondered his next move, rather than the instant uptick in her heartbeat; the odd vibrations coming from her that awakened every cell in his body; the instant priming that had sent him to a cold shower. It didn't work. He was already cold and dead. Any heat came from her and what being in her sphere did to him. It wasn't something he controlled, either. Every portion of her seemed fashioned to gain this exact reaction in him. Pure want, absolute need, unrelenting craving.

She was his mate! She existed...and he'd found her!

How was it possible to be so blessed? So amazingly favored? And yet...how could the fates be so unfair at the same time by keeping her from him? How was it possible she belonged to another man? That wasn't listed in anything Akron had described. Dane had been told if he was really lucky, or if the stars aligned just right, or if every soothsayer he'd visited proved accurate, he'd find his mate, or she'd find him. And together they'd be whole. It wouldn't be deniable or negotiable. On either side. The world would have hope and trust and meaning again.

Dane licked his lips. She shifted slightly, whether at annoyance over the length of time he contemplated his move, or the war of emotions and urgencies he was straining to keep in check. He didn't dare look at her to verify anything.

Pawn, d2 to d4.

He took a move that blocked her and opened access for his queen and bishop. She immediately moved the pawn in front of her rook two spaces forward – a7 to a5. She needed to take more time with her moves! She needed to evaluate and slow things; give him time to control the massive urge to lunge across the table at her, enfold her, gain access to her innermost areas, her most feminine secrets…her perfection.

"Sex and Sunburn," she spoke, interrupting the silence.

"What?" The word was strangled.

"That's the property I want to buy."

Dane picked up his bishop with a hand that shook and slammed it down on space 5b, threatening her queen. He'd also used too much force. The square his bishop occupied cracked right through the center of the marble. She sucked in a breath, as if reading his thoughts. Her heart thumped harder, and faster, drugging his ears with the sound.

Damn.

He lifted his head and glared at the ceiling. This was harder than he'd expected, a hundred times more wondrous, and a thousand times more painful. He reached for the edges of the table and bit his fingers into it, shredding wood.

"So...are you interested in selling?"

Dane lowered his chin, ignoring the game. He looked right at her and fought the reaction hammering through him, to center right at his loins. He narrowed his eyes.

"You ever hear of mates?" His voice was choked. Rough.

"Check...mates?"

"No. Real mates."

"Of course. Socks...have mates. Left. Right."

"Not socks. People. Male to female. Female to male. Or sometimes male to male. Female to female. Whatever. Those kinds of mates."

"I've heard of it."

"You don't believe in it, either?"

"Maybe. Here. This was my move." She lifted the pawn she'd placed on 6c, blocking his bishop.

"How about soul mates?" he asked.

She blew a heavy breath that lifted stray hairs on her forehead. Or his eyes and ears were deceiving him. Her heart rate sped up another notch. Her voice warbled for the slightest moment when she answered, too.

"If...you're playing the lead in a romance play, I'll believe it. Otherwise. No."

"You don't believe there's one being on this planet fated to be with you, mated with you, melding with you? And only you. Forever?"

She gulped. He heard it. His entire body reacted with a lurch toward her. He squelched it. And then she answered with a nonchalance that triggered more reaction.

"Nope. It's illogical. And wasteful. Think about it. If you have a right sock and a left goes missing in the wash, then all you have to do is stick another left sock with it. Simple solution. Right?"

Dane growled. She jumped slightly and lifted wide eyes to his. This wasn't working. He needed to woo her, not scare her. The table edge piece broke into his palm, but a knock on one side of his double door covered it.

"Yes?" He turned his head toward the portal. It was Sven.

"Beg pardon, Dane. You're wanted."

"Handle it."

"Can't. It's Akron. Specifically for you. Only you."

Dane pushed back from the table, taking the piece of wood with him. Her question stopped him.

"You'll be back?"

"Hell couldn't prevent it, *Frja.*"

"You want to make another move first? Or leave me in suspense?"

He leaned over, picked up a pawn, and moved it forward one space. He didn't care which one. It wasn't important.

"That's not a good move. I'm going to take your bishop."

"Take it."

"With a pawn?"

"What does it matter?"

He met her eyes, trying to project everything he felt with the one look. Her heartbeat got faster and louder, her eyes larger and deeper, and then Sven cleared his throat. Dane was at the door in two steps, and hoped she hadn't watched.

Akron had better have something important to say. Damned important. More important than important. Dane shoved the handle on the communication room down with such force the chrome warped.

"Ah. Dane. There you are. Finally."

The huge television in his cabin was projecting a view of desk and the back of a laptop monitor. And a lot of shadow. As usual. A chair was positioned before it. He ignored it and glared at the screen.

"What do you want?"

"Interrupting something?"

"Yeah. Chess."

"In that case, it's obviously a rescue. I have an assignment for you. Hand-picked."

"Just tell me the name's Harper. That's all I need. Harper."

"Now…that's. Just. Odd." Every word was broken into its own sentence, distinct and separate.

"What?"

"I'm surprised. I'm never surprised, Dane…what is your last name this time? Monroe?"

"Morgan."

"Ah yes. The Captain Morgan rum guy. It was Monroe last time, wasn't it? Hard to keep them straight."

"I change my name every fifty years so I can reacquire all my properties. And get new IDs that pass inspection. You know this. The firm handles all the transactions. Can you just give me the guy's name?"

"You already called it. Harper."

Sweet!

A feeling resembling adrenaline filled him. Dane hadn't felt this sort of elation since his very first battle. It electrified and stunned, and lifted him two inches from the floor before he conquered it and settled back. He had to clear his throat to answer.

"Point me in the right direction. I'll have his head to you within an hour."

"It's not a man."

"It's not?"

"I'm relieved to see all is right in my world, Dane. Thank you."

"What are you talking of?"

"Clairvoyance. For just a bit there, I actually thought you'd gained powers to match mine. Glad to see I'm wrong."

"Just give me the hit. I've got things to do."

"That's right. I'm keeping you from an important chess match. Your mark is Evangeline Harper. Twenty-six. She disappeared from your club last night. Don't suppose you've seen her?"

"I'm playing chess with her."

"Sounds too easy. This is why I chose you, actually. Proximity. Just make certain the body's not connected to us."

"I'm not killing her. Cancel the hit."

"You don't cancel hits with the VAL, Dane. We don't give refunds and we don't miss. Handle the assignment or I'll send someone else."

"You can't. She's my mate."

Silence answered that. And then laughter.

"What's so damned funny?"

"You. This. Of all the associates, I'd never put you with an Ivy-league educated woman. Never."

"Thanks." Dane's voice was sarcastic.

"No offense, bud. It's just…you're barbarian to your fingertips, and she—. Well, she doesn't have much of a record to her name. Never steps off the path of civility and righteous behavior. Not even a parking ticket. She probably sings in a church choir. But, we don't pick our mates, do we? No worries. Just take a picture of her looking dead before you change her. I'll need proof of the hit."

"I can't change her. Not yet."

"Why not?"

"She's married to someone else."

Akron burst out laughing again. Dane watched the screen without expression.

"Now, I really have heard everything. This explains your interest in Mister Harper's health, too. Tell you what. I'll do some research. You get me a photo of your mate's death. And try to keep the authorities out of it. Got it?"

"Do I have a choice?"

"Hmm. This is interesting."

"What?"

"Here's a bit of information on a Roderick Dee Harper. Hartford, Connecticut. Deceased. Apparently he died from lingering aftereffects of a shooting. Drive-by. Senseless urban violence. No arrests. No massive insurance pay-out. That's got to hurt the finances. No wonder she's working for these folks. Services were last fall. And look. Here's the listing for a bereaved spouse. What do you know? It's Evangeline Harper, age twenty-five."

"What?" Dane jumped forward, his eyes glued to the screen, while the rest of him felt like fireworks were getting lit on very short fuses, ready to explode.

"You've got access to the internet. You could look this up. It's a matter of public record. Free. Easily available. Accessible to anyone. I'm not even breaking any laws here. Is this her picture?"

The entire screen filled with a newspaper photo, as grainy as the one from the paper earlier. But still his Evangeline.

"She's a widow!" The words were shouted. Joy-filled.

The photo disappeared.

"I want her death photo by sunrise, Dane."

"Whatever," he answered. He was already at the door and flipping the handle.

"Ah…the young."

And with that parting word, the screen went black.

CHAPTER FIVE

Now, why had he moved that pawn and not his bishop?

Vangie leaned forward, examining the board for any possible variant he'd make if she took his bishop. It didn't make sense. His queen didn't have access to anything without a couple of moves she'd have to be blind not to notice. Maybe he was planning to use his other bishop to set up an ambush? Or…maybe his knight?

She stood to appraise it from another angle. The heavy chair didn't shift. It would take effort to shove it against the carpet, and she didn't expend any. She needed to figure out what Dane was setting up. That meant not wasting the time he'd just given her. Or…maybe he'd planned this interruption, to exactly this result - leaving her to stew over possible moves, before he blind-sided her or something.

What was his plan? Her clear move was to take his bishop. Anyone would. It would be an easy slaughter. But that kind of move didn't resemble her opponent at all. Dane didn't appear to be one who did suicide moves. Not if it didn't pay back somewhere. He looked more like the marauding type. Conquering. Taking. Holding. Caressing. Kissing. Molding his nakedness about her on satin sheets...

Get hold of yourself Vangie!

She wasn't going to figure out what that man planned if she couldn't keep her mind on the business at hand, and that meant staying away from contemplation of the physical effect of being near him, breathing the same air, sharing the same space, tingling with awareness of everything he did and said.

"You see?"

She said it aloud and stepped away from the table.

"This is why I detest chess. One move can take hours to figure out. Hours. And it's really going to take an eternity if he doesn't come back soon. *Men.*"

She turned away. Pondering potential moves was a sure recipe for a headache. Surveying the room sounded more promising and interesting. And it was. Dane had an eye for interior decorating. There were a couple of settees gracing one far wall. They looked as overstuffed as the chair. She was tired of sitting. Vangie arched her back in a stretch. The plane ride had been cramped and her seatmate hadn't shut up, and then she'd had to deal with the reality of Dane Morgan. No wonder she was out-of-sorts.

He did something to her. She wasn't a romantic, but that man excited everything in her body, starting the instant she'd locked eyes with him. He sent off solid sexual appeal with every prolonged moment in his company. Just being on the other side of the table heightened everything to the point she was ready to go completely against type, rip her suit off, and jump him. She'd never contemplated a one night stand - never even considered it. And yet…with Dane Morgan…

Heck, it wasn't just being considered, it was a downright fight to suppress the urge. She'd never been wanton. Loose. Passionate. Lustful. Never experienced anything approaching them, but every prolonged moment with Dane…she wasn't just imagining, she was fully fantasizing. And now that he'd gone, leaving her to stew and ponder and evaluate - what was she supposed to do with these elevated hormones?

Ugh.

She was tired, and yet energized simultaneously. It was probably the result of lack of sufficient sustenance. Rest. It had nothing to do with Dane Morgan. It couldn't. Yet, everything felt weak and wrung out. As if she'd been through an emotional experience of some kind. But that was ridiculous. She'd moved a couple of chess pieces, bandied some words, played with double entendre. Yet, still the release from the tension of his presence was physically palpable. Chilling. Deflating.

There was nothing else for it. She could stand here weaving in place while she attempted to ignore her reactions to him…or she could occupy herself. He might have a magazine or at the very least a comic book hidden away, and he really shouldn't leave her alone this long if he didn't want her snooping.

Vangie slid a hand along one of the cabinets against a wall. It looked like it contained wine bottles. Ancient wine bottles. Odd. Dane Morgan didn't look like a wine connoisseur. He looked exactly like a spoiled, rich, extremely pretty, party boy. A chick magnet. The type that turned heads.

As for his banter?

Oh...please.

How did he expect her to give him a decent game of chess? The view was hampering her thought processes, and then his words added to the sensory experience. She couldn't concentrate. She could barely answer him logically. As if he'd really be interested in her. Everything he said and did gave her heart an uptick. But, let's be honest here. She turned men off. Wasn't that what Rod accused her of more than once? That's why she still wore her ring. No reason to turn men off if they didn't approach in the first place.

And the most gorgeous man she'd ever seen wanted to talk about mates? *Not just mates, Vangie...but soul mates?* Maybe when she was a girl she'd believed in true love and soul mates, but now? Not anymore. Real life gave her a reality check. Evangeline Harper and Dane Morgan? Those names didn't belong in the same sentence. And...soul mates? No way. But...wow. Wouldn't that be a dream come true?

Double wow.

Vangie sighed heavily and went back to checking out his cabinets. It was better than her imagination at the moment. She was a business woman conducting a negotiation. She wasn't a siren attempting to seduce a man. Or maybe it was better phrased as an innocent maid being seduced by a god from Mount Olympus?

Dream on, Vangie. Just keep on dreaming...

Next to the wine cabinet was a bookcase. Shoulder-high, with a thick glass front that latched with a little wrought-iron loop. Vangie pulled one door open and lifted out a binder. It was old, looked to be bound with embossed leather, and a bit dusty. She propped it on her hip, lifted the front open, and scanned the pages inside. She might be mistaken, but this looked like a full set of stories that compiled the POSTHUMOUS PAPER OF THE PICKWICK CLUB. Her breath caught at the next page and her eyes went wide. It was a signature. Charles Dickens. 1836. No way. If what she was looking at was true, this collection later became the novel THE PICKWICK PAPERS. And Dane Morgan owned a complete signed first edition?

No way again.

Her hand trembled as she replaced the binder and selected another. This one was even more spectacular. She was looking at a beautifully bound book titled THE MODERN PROMETHEOUS. It didn't have an author listing, but she knew what it was - FRANKENSTEIN. She'd heard of the first printing, but never thought to actually see one. As for actually holding it? It wasn't possible! But here it was. In her arms. It really did have a forward written by Percy Blysshe Shelley. This book had been printed in 1818 with a print run of 505 copies. And on the second page, there was an inscription in extremely poor handwriting.

To one handsome Dane. Mary Shelly, 1839.

Vangie's jaw dropped. Her entire body shook, causing a loose page to fall from somewhere within the pages. She had to set the book reverently atop the bookcase before retrieving the page, and if she'd in any way damaged this, she'd never forgive herself.

It wasn't a page from the book. It was a drawing. Four figures in Regency dress were seated around a table, playing cards. They were easily identified by someone who'd studied literature and spent time getting tested on it. There was Mary Shelley. Her husband, Percy. The poet, Lord Byron. And Dane.

No frickin' way.

Her mind stalled. Her pulse hammered. She couldn't be seeing this correctly. If Dane had a drawing depicting him with the Shelleys and Lord Byron, it couldn't have been him. What was she thinking? He probably didn't even read. Sex and sunburn sounded like his creed, not just the name of his bar.

It was obvious he'd inherited a fortune. It must include lots of priceless items. Dane was probably a normal first name for his family. He had forebears who'd known the value of the printed word and then they kept their books in museum condition. And handsomeness was another obvious legacy. It was in his DNA.

"We have to talk."

Vangie jerked, dropped the picture, and then tried to spin. The carpet height combined with her new heels tripped her. She'd have fallen if Dane hadn't reached out and pulled her right to him, breast to abdomen, hard arms about her back, his mouth just above her forehead.

"I see you found my Byron sketch."

The words rumbled through where she was pressed to him. *Byron sketch?*

"I thought I'd lost it."

"What?"

Her mind wasn't working. It had something to do with how he'd lifted her without a bit of argument on her part, fitting her breasts right against some very hard pecs, while his mouth hovered somewhere at her temple, touching and then sending a riot of goose bumps with every pulse beat against his lips.

"My sketch. Forget it. It doesn't matter, anyway."

"It was in the...book."

"Oh."

"How can you own...something so rare?"

His lips slid, trailing what felt like a kiss to the side of an eye...to her ear. Vangie might as well be melting. Nothing on her was giving him the slightest fight.

"Don't ask me. I can't answer that yet."

"You need...to put me down."

"What? Why?"

He moved his head, matched his forehead to hers and locked gazes. She'd heard of this kind of contact, seen it in movies, but never experienced it. Her heart almost hurt as it lurched, feeling like it closed off her throat.

"Dane...I—"

He grinned, putting little lines about his eyes. She gulped.

"You just called me Dane."

"You...really need to put me down."

"Why?"

"Because…uh. Oh! We're playing chess. And this is against the rules."

He pulled back, granting her a little space to haul in a breath, while this time his grin exposed teeth; long, sharp, fang-like teeth. Evangeline's eyes widened.

"You forgot my heritage, Baby."

"Uh…"

"Viking."

He lifted his brows, creating little creases in his forehead. As if that was supposed to make his argument feasible or do something other than draw her eye there before she moved inexorably back to locking gazes with him.

"You heard me. And believe me. It's all true. We take what we want."

"Take?" *Want?* He couldn't possibly mean that like it sounded.

"I just found out you're not married."

He was sending out too much sensory stimulation for that statement to do other than confuse her. "What?"

"You're widowed. And that means you're mine. All mine."

"That's…just. It's ridiculous. That's what. This is the twenty-first century, Dane."

"I know. All this technology just makes it easier."

"To do what?"

"Viking things. Locate. Pillage. Plunder. Create havoc. Ravish. Satisfy."

"Oh…" *Wow.* She didn't know why she tried to answer. Her voice was missing.

"Don't tell me you've never heard of love at first sight, either?"

"Love?"

He nodded.

"At first sight?"

He nodded again and then tipped his chin down, favoring her with a soul-stealing look that carried fire-starting emissions. The heat seared all the way to her toes and back, before settling along everywhere they were pressed together.

"With…me?"

"Oh yeah."

"You're serious?"

"Dead serious. Pardon the pun."

"Why can't I believe any of this?"

"I don't know. Why?"

"Maybe because…uh. You! You're a babe magnet that looks about…twelve. It would be cradle robbing."

"Twenty-four. Maybe twenty-five. Physically. And what has age to do with love anyway?"

"You—. I mean. You—." Cohesive thought and common sense both evaded her. As did the ability to form words of argument.

"Yes?" His right eyebrow went up. It wasn't helpful.

"You probably have women crawling all over you. Men, too. Twenty-four, seven. And everything in between."

"There's only one woman in my world, *Frja*. One."

Her heart stuttered. She could feel it. "But…we just met."

"Untrue. It's been hours…and I've already waited centuries for you. Centuries."

"Dane, I—"

"What does all this matter? Don't you feel anything for me?"

Every cell that made up her body reacted to him, worse than before. Every word he said just added a skim of cream to the milk.

"This is too fast."

"Darling, it's been an eternity of want, a millennia of loneliness, and a full evening of frustration and rampant need. It's not going fast enough in my opinion."

"Come on, Dane. See sense."

"Speak some."

"I came to talk about your property. That's all I need to—"

"You can have it. Anything you want. It's yours."

"What?"

"Anything I have. It's yours. I promise."

"This is so wrong. On so many levels."

"You're my mate, Evangeline. I recognized you the moment I saw you. I swear it. You don't understand how long I have waited for you. Longed for you. Loved you. It's been an eternity of time. And now you are here. With me. And you're not married as I'd thought. There's nothing wrong in there that I can spot."

"Oh…wow."

The words were moaned. Even to her ears it sounded like a plea. Was it possible? Evangeline Harper, the woman who'd been fully slated as an old widow was going to have her fantasy? Her very own one-night stand?

"Does that mean yes? Please say it means yes. It does! Say it does. Come on, Love. Say it. Please?"

"I don't...carry protection." The words were whispered.

"Protection? You have no need of such a thing! I will protect you! No harm shall ever come to you. Ever. They'd have to go through me first."

His chest tightened, pushing pecs into her breasts, while everything on her supplanted to make room. He was pure male. Dominant. Primal. Angered. And fully ready to defend, guard, and protect.

"I...mean *protection*." Her voice dropped on the word, and if he made her say it, she was going to die of embarrassment.

"I don't follow."

Figures.

Vangie pulled in a breath from the space he gave her, shut her eyes, and still couldn't suppress the blush. "Rubbers, Dane. You know...prophylactics. Why isn't this as easy as they show in those stupid videos? I've never had a-a-a one-night stand. But I know I'm supposed to ask these things."

He snorted. Her eyes opened although she kept them narrowed. After saying the most embarrassing statement of her life, he laughed?

"It's not funny."

"Ah... *Frja*. You are adorable! You call this a one-night stand? I have not been succinct! There is no boundary to us! You do not understand, and if I had the talent for rendering, I've forsaken it. You are the epitome of my reason. The eternity to my forever. The treasure to my search. The universe to my scope. The height to my elevation. The amazement to my wonder. The air to my world. The quintessence of—"

"How old are you again?"

"You see? I've no talent for speech, even when I try. I do better with action."

"If we do this, Dane, I'm not just having sex with you. I'm having sex with everyone you've had sex with. And that's probably an astronomical number."

"What do you mean *if?*" he asked.

CHAPTER SIX

Madmen came in all shapes and sizes. And ages. And looks. The one she faced was a prime example; all brute strength, amazing handsomeness, and demonstrating a pretty extensive vocabulary, too. He still had to be mad. She was Evangeline Harper. Staid. Uptight. Somber. Dispassionate. All business. Critical and Logical.

"I'm serious, Dane."

"Do I not appear serious, as well? I must be rustier than I thought."

"How many women are we talking?"

"What else did you say? We are having sex? Oh no, my sweet. It will not be sex. That I guarantee. We will be making love...for hours. Or what is left of the night, anyway."

"That many women, huh? Any men?"

He rolled his eyes. "There is no amount, *Frja*. There is just you. Only. Don't you listen to one thing I say?"

"You're telling me you've been celibate? Is that it? And you actually expect me to believe it?"

One side of his lip lifted, revealing sharp teeth again. Fangs. That was ridiculous, too. She flicked a

glance there and then back to eyes that were
sparkling with what looked like moisture atop them.
But that was even more ridiculous.

"I'm saying the woman I've waited an eternity
for is here...in my arms, and in my life. The one
woman who can grant me perfection. Bring life
back to my essence. Make me whole again! I'm
talking ecstasy! Fulfillment. Bliss. I cannot
continue! All I know is that if I don't get you into
my bed, and shortly, then I'm going to be ruining a
very expensive chess set over on that table. I don't
know what you're hearing, but this is what I'm
saying."

He maneuvered her chin up, so her view was
paneled ceiling, while what could only be his mouth
touching against her jaw started the most delicious
shivers to reach out and enwrap her. Vangie panted
for breath as he lightly sucked, sliding his mouth
along her jaw line. To the sensitive skin right below
an ear. She tilted her head, allowing him access.

Pain flashed through her throat, followed by fire,
and then the most amazing sensation of pleasure
took its place. Owning her. Claiming her. Sucking
her into a vortex that seemed to gain speed before
her eyes. She told herself she was seeing things. It
was impossible. Completely outside the realm of
reality. As if they were spinning in place. It didn't
help. She slammed her eyes shut on a kaleidoscope
of colors and shapes that meshed into a blur and the
next moment got the sensation of cool air about her
shoulders and neck. As if her jacket had developed
a mind of its own and left her. The release of her
skirt buttons wasn't far behind.

"Dane?"

"Darling."

The murmured endearment made her heart stutter. As well as the motion of his mouth at her neck, alternately sucking and licking and sending ecstasy that seemed to increase in volume and content with every passing second.

"You...must stop. I mean we. We...must stop."

"Command me something easier to accomplish. Like...existing. Command me to cease that."

"Dane."

"I know. I sound mad. But you don't understand, and despite all my years and wasted effort, I've yet to develop enough talent with words to explain it. I've got just this one chance...for what's left of the night. To convince you. That's all the fates have decreed, blast them, anyway!"

"Convince me...of what?"

"My love."

The word was whispered and yet sought out every corner of the space. It carried reverence and something else. A sob of sound. Her heart palpitated as his entire frame began shaking. She rolled a breath through her lips that was supposed to portend an argument, but instead it sounded needy and grasping and desirous. And nothing at all like her.

"You see what I am up against? And you ask me to stop? Pray ask something I can grant."

Vangie slit an eye open. They weren't in his study. Or whatever that cabin was called. The sight of more paneling met her eye, lit by a myriad of candles, and then a huge four-poster bed. And if she turned her head to check, she knew she'd see red satin sheet. The sensation of cool fabric met her back, chilling for the barest moment before turning warm. Heated. Slick. Against naked skin.

Hers.

"How did we get here?"

"I have a great gift of dexterity, my love."

"Where are my clothes?"

She was pulling on the sheets trying to cover herself, and he was there at every move to stop her, showing off his dexterity, and then he lowered his head, took her lips, and turned it to complete exposure. Vangie writhed on the sheets, her legs wrapping about his denim covered lower limbs, while her hands delved beneath his shirt, sliding along the muscled smoothness of his belly. Chest. Back to his waistband. Again. Her palms created a friction of sparks wherever they touched. And then he moved, getting to his hands and knees, separating from her kiss as he crawled back off the mattress, taking the top covers with him.

"Don't leave me!"

"Are you crazed? I'd as soon hammer a stake through my own heart."

"Then give me back some cover."

"I cannot do that, my Evangeline. I wish to see. I want to worship. Adore. You are beautiful, you know that? So beautiful. So warm! So sweet. Your smell! Your…taste! I cannot explain how it feels."

"Dane—."

"Pray, do not stop me. I'm on a roll. Oh! I've a glib tongue when it matters. At least, that's what Percy used to accuse. And trust me, my love. Right here and right now – it matters. More than I can describe."

"Percy?"

He yanked the t-shirt off, displaying glorious muscle that wasn't as tanned as the rest of him. That was odd. Sun worshipping surfer dudes usually wore nothing but swim trunks. Tan lines like his had to be a complete faux pas on the beach. But then he cancelled out every errant thought by putting his hands on his hips, lowering his jaw, and sending a look at her that made her jerk visibly.

"Oh...wow." Her sigh carried every bit of feminine appreciation. There wasn't any way to hide it.

"What?"

He reached upward, putting definition to all that muscle, as if preening for her. And if she hadn't already thought him the best looking man on the planet, she was blind.

"What? Come on, Dane. You're stunning. And you know it."

"It's all for you, Baby. All. Forever. Yours."

He flipped the top button of his denims open and pulled until the zipper trailed apart. Her mouth dropped open. He had the most cut lower abdomen she'd ever seen, too. Even on an Olympic swimmer.

"How did you get so...ripped?"

"You like?"

"Dane."

He grinned and lifted his jaw. "You have a way of chastising with just the mention of my name. I adore it, too. Never change. Okay?"

"Are you going to answer the question?"

"Oh. Yes. I look this way because I didn't spend my growing years on my ass playing video games as they do now. Things were a bit different. And I was the active sort."

"You played sports?"

"Not played, exactly. It was more like…work."

"Work? Did you grow up on a farm? You tossed a lot of hay or something?"

"Actually, I misspoke. It was more like play. But with competition. I spent a lot of years rowing. A lot."

"Rowing?"

"Yes. Rowing. With oars."

"You were on a rowing team? That explains a lot."

"Once I earned the position, yes. But first I had to successfully learn how to dodge things."

"What…like dodge ball?"

"More like spears and javelins. Once I learned how to dodge, then it was catching and tossing back. I got very good at it. Very good. I already told you of my dexterity. I don't have many scars. I was the youngest to earn a position at an oar."

"How young?"

"Twelve."

Her eyes went wide to match her mouth. "What kind of childhood did you have? And where on earth were you raised? And who would do such a thing?"

"We will have to discuss that later, too. Fair?" And without awaiting her answer, he shoved his pants to the floor.

Fair? Hell no. The man was completely unfair. He knew that, too. It was in the look on his face. Vangie wasn't an innocent, but Dane was more than she expected and entirely more than she knew how to handle. But oh! How she wanted to try! She licked her lips, trembled with what had to be yearning and longing and craving and desiring, and everything she'd once fantasized about. She looked up at his face.

"What?" He wasn't just preening. He was on full display. And proud of it.

"You! And uh...you. Oh my stars. You're so...uh—"

He lunged onto the bed beside her, denting the mattress with his weight as well as making the entire structure shake with the force of his entrance.

"I am your mate, *Frja*. I will not harm you."

"Harm me?"

The man wasn't just a failure with words. He didn't read expressions well, either. As for body language? Her entire being seemed more concerned with texture and sensory experience. It wasn't a need; it was an all-consuming hunger of need. Want. Ache. To hell with words and explanation. A well-spring of desire spread luminous wanton through her limbs.

"I swear it. It would be akin to desecration when I wish only to worship."

"Worship?"

"You are impossible to convince with words! Someone has made you mistrust everything said to you. I shall just have to resort to my heritage."

With that, he pulled her right against him and seized her mouth with his.

Skin of an impossible texture and feel touched all along her, absorbing every minute lunge she made against it. Tendrils of scented warmth laced about them, binding them together with invisible strength. Inflexibility. Completeness. The sensation of a bed disappeared, replaced by a meshed web of support that braced her every breath, captured her every sigh, and pressured her every pore…fully against him. Vangie couldn't get enough of the sensation!

It was her legs entwining about him, her throat the one moaning, her arms the ones stealing beneath him to clasp behind his back, mashing her breasts against his chest.

Vangie melded with him, her entire being crying out for a joining with him. Fully. Completely. Her legs moved upward with little lurches, going up past his buttocks to his lower back, wrapping about him to press her apex against his. Willing their consummation. Begging for it. Careening toward it. She felt his chuckle of amusement, a sting at her mouth, and then the taste of blood…and with it came a spectacular lightning flash of complete light and joy and bliss.

She pulled away to cry aloud with joy at it, not even noting how he'd moved to her neck again, piercing, before sucking and pulling at her flesh. A red haze washed about them, filling the enclosure with more than warmth. Burning fire. Scorching heat.

"My love! My mate! My *Frja*!"

Whispers accompanied the movement of his mouth along her neck, back to her mouth, and with the kiss, he shoved his rod fully into her, impaling her on such strength and size that fireworks might as well be exploding throughout the chamber, lit from the fuse he started. The eruption of sensation was more than she could believe. It consumed her, taking her to another realm of existence that was too beautiful to contain. Vangie pulled away from the kiss, arching her head back in order to allow the cry of ecstasy space for sound, loud and with perfect clarity. It didn't quit until her breath ran out. She'd never felt such abandonment, such fulfillment, such satiation, such joy. Wonder. Amazement. There wasn't one thing frigid about any of it.

Blue eyes were waiting for her when she brought her head back down, the lashes shadowing them into dark pools of depth. Mystery. Secrecy. Thrill.

"Wow."

She whispered it, and got a crooked smile in reply. Her heart contracted in a painful beat before going back to a ratcheted degree, seeming to fill her ears with a thumping that added to the cacophony about them. Vangie was the one lunging back to connect her lips to his again, and this time, it wasn't blood she tasted, but pure nectar. An aura filled with light, and joy, and complete delight cocooned them. It added to the melee of sounds and images and sensations, and through it all, Dane continually moved; lifting onto his arms in order to gain better positioning, hammering his loins against hers, his shaft filling her over and over, his essence melding with hers. Deep and intense. Hard and full. Faster. Thicker.

More.

Glimmers of intensity became all-out tremors of need, and those gave way to eruptions of complete orgasmic ecstasy, and each one carried her cries of joy to the world. Again, and again, and so many times, she lost count, and then something changed. His rhythm altered, going to a harder, faster, and tighter degree, while everything on his body tautened,   resembling   flesh-wrapped   iron everywhere she clung, and then he went stock still, flinging his head back to send an unearthly groan that trembled as it hung in the air. Vangie watched as he stayed in that position, his entire body shaking until the mattress shifted beneath them. And then he slackened, brought his head back down and pierced her rapt gaze with his.

"My… *Frja*."

She could've asked what that endearment meant, but it didn't matter. The look of absolute adoration on his face, combined with the intensity deep in his eyes didn't have another definition. She was looking at love. And that's when the tears started.

CHAPTER SEVEN

He'd made her cry?

Dane twisted onto his back, taking her with him, while spurts of bliss continued to radiate from where their loins still joined. Fulfillment and complete satisfaction filled him, sent there with her every pulse beat. He could identify every feature of the room. Light. Sound. Smell. Wonder. He'd never felt as he did right now. Ever. Reality seemed an eternity away, but it intruded the moment he'd seen her tears.

"I sincerely hope those are tears of joy, Evangeline. If not, we are going to have a severe problem, you and me."

He sent the remark to the ceiling above them. She moved her head, hopefully to nod. He hoped it was a nod!

"Is that a yes?"

She moved her head again, and he pulled her closer, bringing her fully atop him so he could prolong the experience of being at one with her. Melded. Fitted. Combined. And for these precious few moments in an eternity of them, it felt like they still were. Words completely failed him at the extent of what he'd just been gifted.

He'd found his mate! She was everything he'd dreamt of and more! Perfection. Harmony. The planet might have stopped revolving for all he cared. Time could cease. Truth disappear. Facts wane. They were nothing compared to the reality that was his dead heart picking up every beat from hers, sending pulse noise to his ears.

He hadn't changed her. Not yet. When it came down to it, he found he couldn't force her. He loved her too much! He wanted her to return it. And for that he needed time! More than the three hours or so left of the night. He wordlessly sent that request to the span of space above him, as well. Look at him; begging the fates for more of the one commodity that had seemed eternal. It was unbelievable.

Her hair was loose about them. He couldn't remember pulling hairpins, but there wasn't much clarity during that gray area when he'd been focused on getting her naked skin against his. Dane frowned slightly. He'd unbuttoned her suit jacket, blouse, bra…pulled off her skirt. There wasn't recollection to where her pantyhose and other items might be, and nothing about hairpins. Didn't matter. He could be atop them for all he cared. Dane lifted a lock of hair and separated the strands between his fingers, watching it divide. Glossy. Clean. Fine.

Everything about her was absolute, stunning perfection.

There was a lot to do and nothing on him wanted to start. He had to get the ship moving. Stay off radar. Hide her from Akron while he located those who'd ordered her death so he could return the favor. It wouldn't be easy. She appeared innocuous, more like a day-trader than an assassin's mark. He might have to call in a favor from the Crusader knight, Invaris. Or that Leonard fellow. As much as Dane distrusted humans, Len was all right. Trustworthy. Good shot. Great at the little details.

She'd ceased crying if the little sniffles were accurate. Thank goodness. He was clueless about an emotional female. He should probably offer and then find tissues. Or something. She sighed softly, touching his neck with just a hint of air. The reaction went all the way through him, as ripples of goose bumps were followed by tremors. And if the physical manifestations he'd been gifted with included crying, they were really going to have trouble.

Dane settled her hair back, stroking it into place on a shoulder before moving his hand lower, meandering about a back and the curve of buttocks that were everything feminine and soft, and perfect.

"Thank you."

Her whisper stopped his explorations. He didn't know how to answer, so he didn't. He simply froze in place.

"I—I didn't know. I mean...I knew. I did. I just didn't believe it."

"What?" Good. His voice was still low and masculine-sounding. Not a bit of emotion attached to it.

"I didn't know...that making love could be so...you know. Wonderful. Amazing. I mean, it's just... *wow*."

If he still possessed a spirit, it was soaring, elevated beyond magnificence, hovering atop joy.

The sensation transferred to his entire body, lifting them both a fraction before he caught it and collapsed back. She'd never understand. Not yet. He didn't want to spoil a thing by speaking of curses and vampirism. Death and rebirth.

"You?"

He grunted and she lifted her head to look at him. The moment she did, he moved his gaze to the ceiling instead. His emotions were too raw. What she'd given him was too vast. Too new. Too unbelievable.

"Was it…good for you, too? Oh, geez. What a lame cliché."

He licked his lips, tasting dried blood, jerked slightly at the intensity that flared all along him, and then moved his eyes to hers.

"You are everything to me, *Frja*."

"What does that word mean?"

" *Frja?* She is the goddess of love. Of perfection. From the old country."

"Oh, no way."

"You don't believe my words? Or the adoration you evoke in me?"

He reached out with a finger and traced it down her nose to her mouth, using it to outline her lower lip. The tremble that scored her frame transferred right into his, making him lurch slightly. He'd never felt that sort of thing, either.

"I am not perfect. Nobody is."

"You're difficult to convince. Ever. Always. Is that it?"

"I have cellulite."

"You're very funny. You know that?"

"I'm serious. I'd get lipo to remove it, but…well. Everything costs money."

"You do not use surgery on perfection, *Frja*."

"You need glasses, Dane. I swear."

"I speak, but I must not be saying the right words. Evangeline, please. You are my mate. My woman. The only woman for me. Ever. I swear it."

"Dane—"

He placed his finger atop her lips, interrupting her. "You have the ability to change the very elements about me. I'm unable to see anything other than perfection when I look at you. Do you understand? To me, you're not just wonder and beauty; you are the epitome of them. A goddess among mere mortals. If I falter, it's due to my fear at failing to show the proper homage."

"Wow. You're quite the player, aren't you?"

Dane's face fell. "You disbelieve me?"

"Of course."

"But, why?"

"Because…oh, I don't know. Look around you. Look at you. I mean, seriously. You're an absolute babe. Amazingly cut. Hard. Muscled. Gorgeous. Uh…I mean, really. Look. I don't even need to factor in that you're a bazillionaire. You have to scrape women off. I'm just one in a continual chorus line of them. You probably notch the bed post around here somewhere."

He could guess who'd messed with her self-esteem, and the only reason he wasn't killing Mister Harper was because the bastard was already dead. Dane moved both hands to her upper arms, held her for the roll that placed him atop her, still fully sheathed between her legs. And then he lowered his chin and growled. He tried to keep control of it, but the sound still made the air about them pulsate.

"Oh. Yeah. Don't let me forget to add that part."

"What…part?"

"The vampire side."

Dane went perfectly still as his eyes widened.

"What? I wasn't supposed to notice? Oh, come on. You even had your teeth fixed. I can't imagine why. You already have women hooked just by showing up somewhere. I'm going to guess you needed to reel them in by adding sinfully sexy to your portfolio. That's why you paid for tooth alterations, isn't it? And I have to tell you. It was a waste of money. They look fake."

"Nobody calls me a fraud," he informed her.

"Add me to that. I didn't say it, either."

"You infer it." He narrowed his eyes.

"Let's just say….it's hard to believe your sincerity. To a woman you just…uh, you know…met."

"A woman I just made love to. Or are you going to deny that, too?" He pushed his groin into hers so she'd have no doubt about meaning.

"Love and lust are two different things, Dane. And I'm full of clichés tonight, aren't I?"

"Why do you keep trying to turn this into something superficial and light? I'm completely serious and yet you mock me. I'm at a loss. What can I say to convince you?"

She tipped her head slightly and considered him, slipped a tongue onto her lips to moisten them, smiled slowly at him while batting her eyelashes. That look had a devious tint to it.

"Marry me."

"Okay."

"Without a pre-nup."

"Okay."

"In the morning."

"Uh…"

"You see?" Now her smile wasn't remotely devious. It was triumphal.

"See what?"

"You and me. And all this mates-for-life talk. It's not real. It's nice. Don't get me wrong. It's more than nice. And fun. You showed me just how much fun. But it's not real."

"I never said anything about for life," he replied.

"Oh. That's right. You didn't. You should probably let me up, so I can get dressed and check into my hotel. I also have to contact the people who want your property before they send out the National Guard or something."

"You can't just bed me and then leave me."

"That's my line, Dane."

"Tomorrow. I mean, today. Sundown."

"What?"

"I'm marrying you. At sundown. No. Better make it midnight."

"You don't have to marry me, Dane. It was a test. You failed."

"What? How can I fail a test if I don't know the rules?"

"Welcome to the war of the sexes, Dane Morgan. By the way, I think you've taken the naïve party boy schtick a bit too far. Give it a rest and let me up. I need to make a call. I don't want someone reporting me as a missing person and then finding me on your yacht. I couldn't handle the embarrassment."

"Are you trying to anger me?"

"Not really…but if it gets me freed, I'm all for it."

Dane pushed to his side and opened his limbs, releasing her. "Don't go too far."

He watched her roll off the bed, trying to take the sheet with her. She was totally wrong about her body. There wasn't a hint of cellulite to mar any of her perfection. She looked luscious, curvy, soft, and wholly womanly. She knelt out of view. He sat to watch her sort through the pile of clothing on the floor.

"I'm on a ship, and I can't find my clothes. How am I leaving? Where did you put my purse?"

Dane scrunched an eye. Pondered it. And then shook his head. The purse was part of that gray area he'd suffered.

"You can't keep me captive by hiding my cell phone, Dane."

"Use mine."

"Your pockets are empty."

He watched her toss his pants.

"On the dresser."

"Where?"

"Any of them. All of them. I have lots of phones and lots of roaming plans. Go. Pick one."

"I need a robe."

"Oh. I don't think so."

"Jerk."

"Welcome to my war between the sexes," he replied.

She took his t-shirt and pulled it over her head - raising strands of hair with the static - before she stood up, tugged the garment down to the tops of her thighs and then glared at him. It didn't work. She could glare all she liked; he still thought she was adorable. And the t-shirt didn't do much to conceal her. Not the way she'd pulled at it. All that happened was thin cotton molded to every curve. He folded his arms but couldn't move his eyes as she stalked across the room, grabbed one of his phones, and opened it.

She had an excellent memory. He watched her spend a couple of seconds dialing in the air before looking down and punching buttons. Then he had to pretend he couldn't hear everything by pasting a completely blank expression on his face in the event she looked.

"Karakov Enterprises. With a million ways to help you locate what you need."

Karakov? Sounded Russian.

"This is Evangeline Harper calling. Let me speak to Serge, please."

"It's three thirty a.m., Miss Harper. Serge Karakov is not available."

"Tell him I have an answer from Florida. He'll take the call."

She turned to look across at Dane. He regarded her without expression. And then another voice answered, causing her to turn her side to him. That was no great loss. She had a gorgeous profile, too. He was going to have an eternity to watch her and enjoy every moment of it. What a wonderful thought.

"Miss Harper? Miss Evangeline Harper?"

"You told me to call when I had a firm figure for you."

"Uh…yes. That I did. I'm just…surprised to hear from you. That's all."

He was surprised to hear from her. Sounded it, too. That's the clue Dane needed. His lips tipped up before she swiveled in place and almost caught his expression. He blanked it again.

"I'm calling about the property. You know…Sex and Sunburn?"

"You have a price?"

Evangeline put her hand over the receiver. "How much do you want for your property?" she asked Dane.

"I don't have any property," he replied.

"Sex and Sunburn?" She tilted her head as if that would trigger his memory.

"I gave it to you." He grinned. He couldn't possibly hold a blank expression with the way she inhaled through bared teeth.

"Would you be serious?"

He attempted it, but it wasn't easy. It took a few moments to get the blank expression back in place. "It's a cute little place. Brings in a hefty profit and a large crowd. You might not want to sell it. And just think. You'd be my boss. You can even fire me."

"Give me a figure, Dane."

"Invent one, my love. After you marry me, you can do whatever you want with whatever chunk of real estate you want. You might decide to keep that one. We don't really need more crime on the coast, do we?"

She turned her back on him, and spoke softly into the phone. "I'll have to call you back. Apparently, I'm still in negotiations."

"But—"

She clicked the END CALL button, cutting off the man, and her hand was shaking as she put the phone back down. Dane shoved back against the headboard and waited for her next move. One thing he had to give her. This mate of his was an intelligent, feisty woman. It was very entertaining just being around her. And the view was spectacular.

"You just made me look like an idiot," she told his dresser.

"What's one drug lord, more or less?"

Her head snapped around.

"Tell me I'm wrong."

"I never said that. I don't even know for sure."

"But you suspect?"

"I never said that, either."

"You contacted someone about them, didn't you?"

"How did you—? Uh…no. I didn't."

This time he didn't hide the smile. Or the fangs. "Come back to bed, darling. Negotiate with me."

"Dane."

He patted the bed beside him. "Come on, already. The sun will be up soon and then I need to leave you. You can rest. Or make calls. Or I'll send one of my assistants to help. You've got a lavish wedding to plan. Or…you might prefer a beachfront, barefoot-in-the-sand type affair. Either way you need sleep and it sounds like I'm going to be busy…with lawyers and estate people."

"Are you serious, Dane?"

"Yes."

"I mean, really, truly, serious?"

"Yes, yes, and yes."

"Can I trust you?"

"Totally."

"I don't know. Trusting and opening your heart…it's so scary. Things happen. People…die."

He was at her side a second later, cursing the impulse that made him move that rapidly, before folding her into his arms. She turned her nose to the center of his chest and just stood there. Trembling. Fighting tears?

He knew his heart was dead, but the solid thumping radiating from there sure didn't feel like it.

CHAPTER EIGHT

"This is the place?" Dane looked up at stone walls topped with jagged barbed wire, and back at the black clothed man beside him.

"You're looking at the headquarters for Karakov Enterprises, with their million ways to help. Exactly as specified."

"You're sure?"

"You doubt me? Not very flattering, Babyface. And I spent almost five minutes tracking the number from your cell. Vampires. Sheesh."

"Looks deserted."

"Well…I'd expected them to have all the lights on, too, but I guess if you run a crime syndicate, you keep advertising to a minimum. 'Course with a Russian name like theirs, I'd have thought they preferred some ancient eastern estate, but there you go. Florida weather attracts all sorts of people."

"You talk too much."

"Passes time…and you never did tell me what you want with these guys. Aside from the fact they just paid a hefty sum into a VAL account. That wouldn't have anything to do with this little excursion this evening, would it?"

"Did they?"

"Four million. Wire transfer. Came through yesterday. That information took me a lot more than five minutes, by-the-way."

"You didn't tell anyone?"

"The boss doesn't know a thing. Invaris is only slightly wiser. You wanted us off the grid, we're off the grid. So...you going to tell me what's up? Or do I get to continue guessing?"

"Later."

"As long as it's personal. That's all I'm asking. I mean, there's not a member of Karakov Enterprises that doesn't deserve the wrong end of a bullet. Word is they're behind the dead bodies washing ashore. The last guy didn't even make it to the water. They skinned him alive and then fed him to sharks. And I'm rather fond of my epidermis."

"I'm a vampire, Len. They can't touch me."

"Stay close, then. So, hey...back to the question. I'm all for cleaning out a nest of vipers. It's just sweeter if it's personal. It is personal. Right? We're not just sneaking around Akron providing clean-up service for the community?"

They put out a hit on my mate. "Oh, it's personal," Dane finally replied.

"Vampires. I don't know why I ask. I really don't. It's a waste of breath."

"You have a plan?"

"Yeah. Go in. Kill everybody. Leave."

"Good plan."

"The one behind your cell phone call is Serge Karakov. CEO. He'll have an odd heat signature. Elevated temp. He's got leukemia. Just found out. Goes to show that no matter how good-looking and rich you are, everybody gets pain and everybody dies. Nice to know there's a bit of justice to the world, you know? Why am I asking you? You're immortal. You never had a day of pain in your life. Uh…I mean your afterlife."

"I took a spear in the belly, Len."

"Well…that had to hurt, I guess."

"Thanks for the warning. I owe you again."

"What?"

"Serge Karakov's blood. It's tainted."

"You planning on doing a little take-out, are you?"

"No time. I have an appointment at midnight. Can't be all bloodied. I might even have to don a tux."

"I'm not asking. I don't care if you're escorting Miss America down a catwalk. But with that kind of timeline, you'd better quit interrupting me and listen up. We've got more than one target. Apparently, Serge likes to keep the entire board of directors close to him. They're partying somewhere behind that monstrosity of a wall. Odd. I thought every lavish estate in the Keys was open and airy, and had million-dollar curb appeal. This one's more like a thousand year old fortress. If I wasn't looking it over, I wouldn't believe it."

"Five hundred. Maybe."

"No way. Not in the Keys. If that was real, we'd have archeologists swarming the place."

"It's real. Early sixteenth century. Maybe later."

"Right."

"You don't know your own history?"

"Unlike present company, I wasn't there at the time."

Dane smirked before answering. "Spanish conquistador Juan Ponce de Leon discovered the state in 1513. He thought he'd found another island. The crown knighted him and granted him governorship of the entire peninsula. *If* he could hold it. Building a fortress like this one could hold it."

"Oh...come on. That's pure speculation. Karakov Enterprises probably had that chunk of stone designed, and constructed, and purposely aged. For the effect on visitors."

"Nope. But it's been updated."

"Oh, I guarantee it's updated. You hear that hum? That's electricity. Early twentieth century invention. And he says I don't know my history."

"Nineteenth."

Len rolled the curse through his lips. "It'd be easier to take you seriously if you looked old enough to drink...Babyface."

"I'm twenty-four. Maybe twenty-five."

"Maybe? How do you lose count of your age?"

Dane looked over at the man. "You ever work a Viking long-ship?"

"Not recently."

"Trust me. Every day's the same and they're all shit. Easy to lose track of all kinds of things. Land. Food. Sleep. Time."

"Sorry I asked."

Dane looked back to the fortress wall. "You know how many?"

"How many what? Years? Conquistadors? Long-ships?"

"Targets." Dane said it through clenched teeth. He had to remind himself that Len was good. That's why anybody put up with him. The man was more than good. He had perfectly honed skills.

"The board of directors is an eight member unit. All Karakov relatives. They keep it in the family, and still don't trust each other. Hmm. Whatever happened to family values?"

"We have eight targets?"

"Once you get us over that fourteen foot span of rock, there's an electrified fence. That's the humming noise, remember? They've got 25,000 volts running through it. I don't know about you, but that's enough to fry my ass. So, you'll just have to get me over it, too. Then we'll probably face real humans. With real guns. They're not very friendly, either. They probably shoot pizza delivery guys. That's why I'm pretty much dressed head-to-toe in Kevlar."

"Sixteen."

"What?"

"The walls are sixteen feet."

"Right. Vampires. Got to love them. I'm telling you, one of you needs to develop a sense of humor. And before I turn thirty."

"You're thirty-two."

"No kidding? Well…I'm not getting any younger while you sit out here shooting the breeze. You ready yet?"

Dane grabbed Len's shoulders and jumped, easily leaping the barbed-wire topped wall, landing in thigh-sucking liquid Len forgot to describe, before launching them right over the fence that sparked and sizzled with every drop of swamp muck they dripped on it. Nothing like a grand entrance. Dane landed in a crouch and shoved Len to the ground where the man rolled from bullets that sounded like puffs of air.

He'd forgotten to add in that they had silencers.

A blink later, Dane was behind the first man on the left, ripping through his thorax with a blow. Second man got a crushed vertebra and severed spine. Third one received a compressed skull as his brains separated from his head. The fourth one went down with a bullet hole between his eyes. A glance showed Len already taking down the fifth shooter, as well. Dane nodded at his partner. The guy might talk a lot, but he was a damn good shot.

The ground about Len started spurting dirt as bullets riddled the area again. Dane tagged the shooter from above him, and with a jump went right through the stone walkway. That fellow got his head severed from his shoulders for his trouble. Fresh blood gushed from the neck cavity as he fell, soaking stone and the lower half of Dane's trousers, while the scent triggered impulses he had to restrain. Every muscle in his frame tightened, his canines elongated, while his mouth and throat itched with thirst.

Not yet.

Len was huffing for breath as he reached him, jogging the steps to catch up.

"Holy shit, Babyface. I'm speechless. Death and dismemberment must be part of your Viking training? Yes?"

"No."

"Looks pretty barbaric. You sure?"

Dane raised bloodied hands. "Nothing but bare hands."

"Better and better. You're more in a Berserker mode. What a great idea for a video game! Remind me later. We got work to do. You spot him, yet?"

Len pulled night goggles from around his throat and adjusted them. Dane narrowed his eyes and scanned stone, seeing heat tracings in several locations.

"There's a lot more than eight," he remarked.

"Sue me."

"I'd rather reward you. You use steroids?"

"No. And what the hell does that matter?"

"Has an effect like Nitrous Oxide, only not near as fun. When I change you, I don't want to be riddled with laughter for hours afterward."

"Whoa. Hold on there, Babyface. I don't want to be changed. Not yet, anyway. I like living day to day. Honest."

"You change your mind, start feeling old age, you let me know. Fair?"

Another round of bullets peppered the rock about them. Dane shoved Len behind him until the fellow ran out. And then their attacker tossed a long knife. Dane caught it and launched it right back, pegging the guy in the throat. They both watched as the man grabbed his neck and plummeted to the ground.

"Reflex," he remarked in the dead silence that followed.

"That was pretty amazing. Truly. Frickin'. Amazing."

"Nice to know I can still do it."

"What?"

"Part of my upbringing. Dodge and throw. Forget it. You spot him, yet?"

"I've got three in that tower. None of them Mister Heat. You?"

"No. I'll handle the main house. I'll be busy. You get in trouble, you call."

"Oh. I'll be in full-bore screaming. You just keep your ears—"

The last bit was lost as Dane jumped the parapet and slammed through double wooden doors, splintering the bolt that had barred them. Through the blizzard of slivers and dust, he swiped through one man's chest, ripped another man's arms off, and used them to bat the next fellow's skull into the wall before putting the armless fellow out of his misery. The screams brought more footsteps, and Dane turned into a smear of movement, slashing through flesh and severing bone, until the amount of blood running down the walls called to every atom of his existence. Every sense hammered need through him.

Not just yet.

They were using unsilenced guns somewhere. Gunfire sound cut through the scene of carnage as Dane just stood there, head lowered, teeth elongated, eyes narrowed and deadly. The only trace of heat came from the newly deceased, and then he caught a glimpse of warmth and color, shimmering from down a hall. He took off at a run that sent him to the end of the hall and up a spiral staircase.

The figure blocking his way was a martial arts enthusiast. And he was large. Cocky. Settled into an aggressive stance. Waste of time. Dane was going to be late to his nuptials. Dane took a moment to lock gazes before slamming both palms into the guy's chest, right through the defensive motion of his arms. Martial Arts slammed into a wall, breaking most of his bones and liquefying the organs that resisted. Dane was right with him, holding his shoulders in place as the guy gasped his last breath. It was visceral. Sensory. The near-taste called him, the aroma taunted, and need for sustenance almost overtook him. Dane was just slicing a fang through Martial Arts throat when a blade glanced off the rock at his cheek.

A snarl accompanied his pivot, and then his flight, streaking into a moonlit enclave where a slight figure stood, eyes wide and hands to his cheeks. He really didn't need to ask. The fellow's heat signature already had him identified. 99.7 degrees. Fahrenheit. Serge Karakov. CEO.

Dane put his head back and howled the satisfaction into the room. The sound echoed and re-echoed, carrying every bit of his rage with it. Even in the dimness, it was easy to see the man blanch. Dane took a step closer, ignoring how the room warped, shifting slightly as if to encase and entrap him. Little flickers of numbness rose from the floor about his feet, wrapping about his ankles and lower legs, hampering his movements.

"What the hell are you?"

"Your worst nightmare."

Dane opened his mouth wide, revealing blood-enhanced, razor-sharp fangs. The result was exactly what he expected, as the man backed into a stone slab jutting from the floor and then rounded it, as if it would save him. The oddity of the room increased. Invisible flicks of pain started radiating from the walls, carrying a touch of a whip. Dane flinched as each one landed, slicing flesh, and bringing burn. But there was nothing there. He concentrated on the man quivering before him, rather than psychedelic effects that couldn't possibly be happening.

"Vampires…really exist? I don't believe it."

"You put out a hit on the wrong party, Karakov. My mate."

"Oh, shit. Evangeline Harper?"

Another step and he'd have the weasel's throat gripped in his hands, choking the life from him. But that step didn't come. The numbness had spread. Dane glanced to the floor, where nothing but tile menaced him. But then the tile changed, splitting to reveal an opening of solid black. Dane went airborne, exerting energy on hovering atop the opening that just kept getting larger and larger, reaching out with invisible tentacles to suck him down into it. That's when he knew.

He was on consecrated ground.

"Len! Help me! Len!"

His voice hadn't the volume or heft of his earlier yell. It sounded as weak as he felt. Pitiful. Serge Karakov added to the experience by sliding to his buttocks atop the altar stone, just sitting there, watching. The abyss enlarged, starting to rotate in a circular motion, growing blacker and deeper, creating a vortex that sucked at every limb. Dane struggled against it. Twisted. Fought. This couldn't be happening! Not now. He'd sometimes thought of real death; of leaving this existence for the next, putting an end to the loneliness…but not now. He couldn't perish now! Not when he'd finally found everything that made even an afterlife worth living!

Evangeline!

His mind cried it for him. His feet might as well be entangled with bonds of iron. There wasn't any flex to the power holding him, pulling him down into oblivion, without even a chance to see her again. He'd never again speak of his love. Never have the chance to prove it. His chest was a solid cage of hurt that just kept getting worse. Because he was doing exactly what everyone else did to her.

He was leaving, too.

"Dane?"

Her voice arced through the darkness, separating the field of black closing in on him, and for a moment there, he thought he saw her. His beautiful, perfect Evangeline, her hands reaching out for him, grasping and then holding, her efforts doing little to alter the morass of black whirling about him. He'd thank the gods later. He could tell her why he wasn't there for her.

"I'm sorry, *Frja*. I—."

"You're late for our wedding."

"Evangeline?" *Damn weight.* The name was broken. The pressure surrounding him was reaching chest crushing volume.

"Call me girl names later."

"Len?"

"In the flesh. Which is more than I can say for you. Looks like I got here right in time. You're all smoke with just a little teeny light in the center. So, get a move on. Double time."

"How?"

"Grab my hand. You need an invitation?"

Len's fingers tightened, inexorably hauling Dane from the black hole of nothingness. The room slowly came back into focus, the floor settling back into tile, the walls into rock. Dane stood in the center of a mass of shadow that finished rotating and then dissipated at his feet. He had to blink against the sudden onslaught of brightness. Len dropped his hand.

"You in, then? Good thing I came to check on you. Vampires. Sheesh. Just when you least expect it, they need rescuing."

"This is…consecrated ground," Dane mumbled.

"Shouldn't be. Don't they have to unconsecrated sites before selling them? Or something? Must have had some lingering effects. Drastic ones. You look all right now. Oh shut up, Karakov, or I'll help you fall on a knife."

"You could be right." Dane stretched both arms wide, lifted off the floor, hovered a few inches above it. Nothing happened.

"Why can't bad guys have nice mansions with large swimming pools and hot and cold running blondes? That would be preferable to an ancient fortress with its very own chapel. You probably didn't even know it had one, did—? Oh, shit!"

The sound of a gunshot echoed through the chamber. Dane dropped and watched Serge's body fall off the back of the stone slab. Len pitched a revolver after it. Then he looked over and shrugged.

"Uh…suicide."

"Right."

"If you'd look close, you'll notice the guy has a pretty sharp wooden stake in his hand. Don't know where he got it. Or how. And I'm not telling where he was aiming, either. You figure it out."

"Suicide works for me," Dane replied.

"So. You about ready? I'm thinking we'd better get a move on. Wait a sec. I'll just put in a 911 call…from my convenient non-traceable, throwaway, cell phone. I really love these things, don't you?" The silence was interrupted by the sound of buttons and then an operator's voice. Len waited for a count of three before hitting the mute button and pitching the phone onto Serge Karakov's corpse. "That's it. We're done here. Move your ass, already. We got a boat to catch. Oh! Try and get your powers back before we reach the barricades. It'll be easier."

CHAPTER NINE

The lights went out at five minutes after twelve. Not before. Not midnight. After. Five minutes after. She'd known it was too good to be true, but that didn't make it easier, and if she cried she was going to make all this eyeliner and mascara run. Damn men! Damn really gorgeous men! And totally damn Dane Morgan and his lying tongue!

Evangeline lifted her head from the table as pitch black descended on the room. The wedding finery she'd picked out itched and it was too tight. No. That wasn't true. It itched because she was wearing a little, red lace demi-bra, matching thong, and lace-edged thigh-high silk stockings beneath the peach shaded gown. That's what itched and reminded, adding to her self-flagellation. She'd rarely been so taken in. That's what came of opening her heart; cracking it a little, because she'd trusted a man who set her senses soaring, her hormones into overdrive, and her emotions to a whole new realm.

That just made the drop harder. And she was not going to cry!

"Miss Evangeline Harper?"

She jumped as a voice spoke from somewhere behind her, soothing and yet frightening in a simultaneous blend of sound. She'd never heard such a timbre, as if cavernous depths perfectly melded with soaring heights to create a ripple effect. The shivers on her body evidenced exactly how much ripple. One of the candles in her candelabra flickered into a weak spot of light, beckoning a glance.

"Yes?" Her voice was barely audible. Whispered.

"My name is Akron."

The candle flame flickered.

"Akron." She repeated it with a bland tone that didn't resemble her at all. Vangie shook her head, cleared her throat, and started over. "Do I know you?"

"Not yet. But you will. You worry needlessly, you know. He'll be here."

"Who?"

"Dane Monroe. I mean, Morgan."

"You know where he is?" Evangeline swiveled on the chair and narrowed her eyes. She couldn't see anything beyond the scope of candle light. And the voice seemed to encompass the entire room.

"Of course."

"He sent you?"

"Not…exactly."

"Then, how do you know whether he'll be here or not?"

"Opinionated. Strong. Brave. And smart. Tell Dane I approve when he gets here, will you?"

"What?"

"His union with you. I heartily approve. Even if he didn't follow orders."

"Follow orders? Are you his boss? Or…something along that line?"

"Oh, no. Not me. We're all self-employed. But he didn't follow the creed. I know why. He was right to do so. Tell him that, too, when he gets here, will you?"

"What makes you so sure he's coming? It's already past midnight."

"I've known him a very long time, Miss Harper. Very long. There isn't a man with more dedication and integrity in him. He's steeped in them. If he promises you something, it's bankable. And I'm sure he's coming because he told me you're his mate. I believe him. We only get one mate, my dear. One."

Vangie gasped. She couldn't hide it. She ducked her head to hide the emotion that was probably on her face and then lifted one of the peach grosgrain ribbons lacing the corset portion of her gown to pick at it.

"You know much history, Miss Harper?"

"Some."

"How about the dark side? You study that at all?"

"Like what? War? Plague? Famine?"

"Go darker."

Her chin lifted. "Alchemy? Uh…genocide?"

"I'm afraid you're in for a bit of a shock, Miss Harper."

"Shock me. Go ahead."

"Your Dane is not twenty-four years old. Or twenty-five, for that matter."

"I knew it! How old is he, then? Nineteen?"

"One thousand and nineteen is closer."

"What?" Her heart stuttered. It matched her voice.

"He's immortal. So am I."

"All right. That's it." Vangie stood so rapidly, the dressing stool fell behind her. Her breath came rapidly with agitation, and there still wasn't anything to see.

"You don't believe me?"

"Of course not. I believe I'm having a really strange dream. It started last night at the Sex and Sunburn club, and it just keeps getting weirder and weirder. And you can tell him that for me when he gets here."

"You're forgetting something, Miss Harper."

"What? My common sense?"

"You're his mate. He only gets one. You. Or didn't he tell you?"

"He said…something along that line. But, it's insane. All of it. Immortality is for fiction readers. And movies. It's not real. The next thing you'll tell me is he's a Viking god or something."

"Actually, he's a vampire."

Vangie snorted.

"So am I."

"Do I really have to respond to that?" she asked.

"Go ahead. Say whatever you like. It doesn't alter facts. And it's not going to change your future."

"Excuse me?"

"I'm head of an elite assassin group. The Vampire Assassin League. You've probably never heard of it, but trust me. We're real. Covert. We can be bought for the right amount. We'll kill anyone, but we make them pay. Draining blood is just our sideline. Draining bank accounts is a lot more enervating."

"I—." Her voice just quit. Her heart wasn't just stuttering, anymore. It hurt with every hard thud against her breastbone.

"My firm accepted a contract for you, Miss Harper. Paid in full. From a Serge Karakov. He wants you dead. Apparently, he thought there might be a bit too much speculation attached to him if he handled it in-house. So, he hired us."

"That bastard!"

"I take it you know the man?"

"He was my boss."

"I see. Ah. I hear the craft approaching. Dane's arrival is imminent, and that means I must go. You ready?"

"You're leaving, then?"

"Do you love him, Miss Harper?"

Vangie's eyes closed and her heart stopped. It took a gasp to make it restart again.

"Dane. The man who says you're his mate. Do you love him?"

"I—"

"You're dressed to marry him. I just want to know why. See…I'm a romantic sort. I like to believe true love conquers all. It rights my world, so to speak. So do you? Love him?"

I don't know. Love is so scary.

"I haven't been lucky enough to find my mate, Miss Harper. I may never be lucky enough. So…I have to sit on the sidelines and watch. And dream.

And envy. It's a simple question. Do you love him, or are you marrying him for what he has to offer?"

"I'd never!"

"He's got a lot to offer. Financial security, for one. And there's his physical attributes. I understand he's rather nice-looking."

"What do you mean nice? He's the most handsome thing on the planet. And I was worried over the decade or so of women he's had sex with? Now, you're adding in over a thousand years of uh…practice?"

"Miss Harper. I haven't been clear. Dane is a vampire. Our bodies are dead. So are our emotions. The only thing that can change any of that is finding our mate. You. Finding you gave Dane back what all creatures hanker for. You are the love of his afterlife. His love isn't a lie. Please tell me it's not one-sided. At least give me hope. That's all I'm asking."

I love him. Everything went crystal clear and focused and perfectly calm, while a slight vibration trembled through her with the certainty. It was solid emotion and it was beautiful. Her eyes filled with tears she had to blink away. *I love him!*

She didn't say it aloud, but somehow he heard.

"Good. Very good. You reassure me. You have no idea. Now, close your eyes like a good girl and think of your handsome groom-to-be. I promise not to hurt you."

And the next moment the candle blew out.

o0o

"We're late."

Dane vaulted onto the deck of the ship from the cigar boat, leaving Len to the ladder. He'd gone for speed to reach the yacht, not skill. That gained him sea spray on clothing that was already stained with blood. He had to reach his suite and shower. Or at least change. Otherwise, she might faint if she saw him. He unbuttoned his shirt as he flew, racing the corridor. One flight of steps. Two.

Damn it!

Evangeline stood right in the doorway of his suite, her peach-shaded wedding gown highlighting a figure that already haunted him. There was something different about her. Something deep and illicit. It teased the edges of his sanity, instantly provoking a corporeal response he couldn't fight.

"Dane."

"Uh…"

Words failed him. He watched as she moved a hand to his chest and planted it palm-down on his skin, right above where his heart should be beating. If he had one, and if it wasn't dead. He searched the space between them for her pulse, so he could match it, and found nothing. No beat. No pulse. Nothing he could use to fake a heartbeat.

"We had a visitor while you were out."

"Uh…"

She'd moved somehow. Her body skimmed to the space right in front of his, sending a myriad of sparks that simulated contact. Heat reached out to him. Need pounded right through him. His canines lengthened despite his effort. She was too real. Too physical. Too perfect. Her scent aroused and stimulated as it dragged him nearer. Dane's entire frame lurched toward her without one bit of help from him. Everything on him ratcheted right to full and ready, and completely desirous.

"For the love of—. Whoa. Color me shocked."

Dane pulled Evangeline to him and swiveled to face Len, who slid the last two steps making a lot of noise as he joined them in the passage.

"I knew there was a woman involved! I knew it. And I'm not surprised. You hit the jackpot, Babyface. She's gorgeous."

Dane stiffened.

"What? I'm not supposed to notice a beautiful woman when I see her? Very nice…even if she is a vampire."

"Who is this?" Evangeline asked, her voice low and sultry.

"What did you just say?" Dane asked.

"I said she's beautiful - even if she is dead. No wonder we rushed things. Hi Sweetheart. Name's Leonard. You can call me Len. Everyone else does. So. Where do I change?"

"Change?" she asked.

"Clothes. Change clothes. Around here, a man's got to be specific. I'm going to guess we're having a wedding. And I'm going to hazard I'm the best man. Tell me I'm wrong."

"Did he call you…Babyface?"

The goddess in his arms giggled. And to get that reaction, he didn't care what she called him. "Yeah."

"I like it. It fits."

"Could you two coo later? I've got a shower to take. And a tux to don. Yes?"

Dane swiveled her in his arms, looked down, and caught the slightest tip of fangs from between her lips. "You're…changed?"

"I told you. We had a visitor. We had a long talk. Mainly about you. He said to tell you it's all right. He'd have done the same thing. But a contract's a contract."

"Akron was here?"

"Shit." That was Len. "This means I'm not as sneaky as I think I am. That's crushing to the ego. Truly. I'm going to have to go lick my wounds somewhere."

"No. Everything's fine. She's a vampire. I'm looking at her."

The lightning flash of joy that arced through him took them both off the floor. Len looked very small as he tilted his head toward them and cleared his throat.

"You want me to leave you two alone? I mean, what's one more day of freedom, more or less?"

"Freedom?"

"He's talking marriage, *Frja*. You and me. Together. As one. It'll be forever. I swear."

"I have something to tell you." Her voice went to a whisper as she nuzzled his neck. "It's more than forever. I love you. You hear that, Babyface? I love you."

And with that, she bit him.

-o0o-

About the Author

Jackie is an Alaskan author who crafts full-length Scot Historical novels for Kensington, while moonlighting with her paranormal series: Vampire Assassin league, available in ebook and 2-pack paperbacks. She loves hearing from fans, who can contact her at www.jackieivie.com

Printed in the USA
CPSIA information can be obtained
at www.ICGtesting.com
LVHW021822081123
763357LV00053B/702

9 781939 820082